Doughnuts, Diamonds and

Contents

PROLOGUE

At the annual St. Eves' summer fair, the fragrance of hot doughnuts and burnt sugar scented the balmy evening air, mingling with the deliciously pungent aroma of glistening fried onions waiting to be piled into warm hotdog buns.

Giddy with excitement, children scurried to stand in line, waiting to hand over the pennies in their sweaty hands in exchange for a ride on the bumper cars or a full circuit on the big wheel which dominated the fairground.

The three friends strolled, arm in arm, content to watch the fast rides from afar but stopping to take their turns on the numerous stalls offering chances to win cuddly toys and trinkets of every description.

"Here, hold this, will you? I'm going to have a go on that shooting range." Ava Preston thrust her handbag at Harriett Lawley and strode the short distance to Tony's Targets, taking her place beside a young man who was chatting with the stallholder. He cut his conversation short when he saw her and turned to give her his full attention.

"Evening, Ava. You're looking very lovely, if I may say."

Ava threw him a pointed glare. "No, you may not say. And, if you could bear not to hear the sound of your own voice for a minute, Derek Whittington, perhaps you could stop talking so I can concentrate?"

"Well, pardon me for living." Derek pulled a face and zipped a thumb and index finger across his lips before folding his arms and stepping back to watch.

"Sure you know what you're doin' with that, love?" The stallholder watched Ava handle the air rifle uncertainly.

"Course I do. I just point and shoot, don't I?"

"Sure you wouldn't rather try your luck on the coconut shy?"

Ava turned her glare to the man, cutting him dead mid-chuckle. "I want that teddy bear hanging over there—the big one with the floppy ears—you see if I don't win it. How many targets do I have to hit?"

"If you want that bear, you'll have to hit all six of 'em."

"Right-o." She steadied the rifle against her shoulder and squeezed an eye shut. Pop, pop, pop, pop, pop, pop.

"Well done. You hit one. You've won a rubber duck." Derek congratulated her, his expression droll. "You know you're only supposed to shut *one* eye, don't you?"

Ava opened her mouth to offer a swift retort but he spoke over her. "Would you like me to show you what you're doing wrong?"

"When I want your opinion, Derek Whittington," she snapped, "I'll ask for it, thanks very much." With a toss of her dark curls, she flounced back to her friends. "Honestly, that boy, he thinks he knows everything."

"He's only being friendly, Ava. And, anyway, all you've done all week is talk about him—Derek, this, Derek, that. I thought you liked him?"

The girls stopped momentarily by a crowd of young men responding to the call to, "Step right up and test your strength! If you can ring the bell, you'll win a Strongman tie-pin and cufflinks set, or a cuddly toy for the lady in your life. Come on gents, step up and show us what you're made of!"

Betty Tubbs gazed at a young man as he picked up the heavy wooden mallet. He walked with a limp but there was nothing frail about Patrick Jones. He raised the mallet high above his head and brought it down on the red lever, sending the metal puck shooting up the tower and ringing the bell at the top, prompting a spontaneous round of applause.

"'E's got the strength of Samson, this one! Well done, sir! Come on up and choose a prize."

Patrick threw Betty a grin and a wink as he flexed his biceps, and she turned away, her cheeks flushing.

Ava and Harriet giggled. "Cat got your tongue, Bet? You must be smitten—it's not often you're lost for words. Mind you, he's quite a looker, so it's hardly surprising. Is that the chap you were telling us about?"

"Oh, be quiet!" Betty stuck out her chin and shook back her golden hair. "I hardly know him. My bicycle chain came off last week outside the post office and Patrick was kind enough to stop and ask if I needed help. He moved to St. Eves a few months ago and I've only spoken to him a few times, so I'm hardly smitten."

Continuing their stroll, they were stopped by Derek Whittington blocking their path.

"So, you going to stop playing hard to get and do me the honour of coming out with me next Saturday, Ava Preston?" He hung back from his friends as they sauntered past.

Ava attempted to walk on but Derek held his ground, walking backwards in front of her. She stopped and crossed her arms, tapping an impatient foot as she looked him up and down. "Hmpf. Well, I *might* consider it but *only* if you're on your best behaviour. No funny business, alright? I'll be ready and waiting at six o' clock. That's what we said, isn't it? And if you're just *one* minute late," she wagged an index finger in front of his face, "don't even bother knocking on the door.

Derek clicked his heels together and saluted her with a grin. "Don't worry, I won't be late."

Harriett shook her head as she watched him catch up to his friends.

"Honestly, Ava. One minute you're jumping down his throat, the next you're making arrangements to go out with him. Are you going to the cinema?"

"No. We're going dancing with a crowd from his ballroom club. I thought the cinema would be too awkward. You know, where would we sit? If we sit in the back row, he might think I'm...well, you know...*that* kind of girl, and if we sit anywhere else, we won't be able to whisper to each other all through the film."

Betty jumped as she felt a tap on her shoulder.

"Here, this is for you."

She turned to find herself face-to-face with a large toy poodle. Patrick Jones poked his head out from behind it and beamed an impish grin. Her cheeks flushed and her mouth went dry. "What's that?"

"Er, well, obviously, it's a stuffed toy. For you. I mean, I won it for you on the Strongman Challenge."

"What for?" Her eyes sought out her shoes.

"Because I thought you'd like it." Patrick scratched his head.

"Yes, I do, but I didn't need you to win it for me." Betty raised her chin, still not meeting his eye. "Look, thank you, it was very kind, but I don't accept gifts from virtual strangers. Now, please stop bothering me." She linked her arms though Ava's and Harriett's. "Come on girls, let's go and get some candy floss."

As they walked away, Harriett turned back to see Patrick staring after them, a confused crease at his brow and the stuffed toy hanging dejectedly from his hand. She waited until he was out of earshot.

"Honestly, Bet. You could try to be a bit more pleasant, you know."

"It's alright for you," Betty huffed. "You've both been out with a few boys. I haven't. I don't know what I'm supposed to do." She held a hand to her cheek, its heat a reflection of her embarrassment.

"What d'you mean, what you're "supposed to do"?" said Ava. "There aren't any rules set in stone, you know, although being nice is a good place to start."

"Erm, have *you* ever thought of taking your own advice, Ava?" Harriett arched a brow. "Talk about pot, kettle and black."

Betty exhaled sharply and picked a clump of candy floss from its stick. "It's not that I don't *like* him, I just don't know what to *say* to him—I always get so tongue-tied—so I think it's best we don't take things any further and just stay friends."

"Somehow, I don't think that's going to be a problem," said Harriett. "I should think you've well and truly put an end to any more romantic gestures he might have been planning. Poor Patrick."

"Oooh, look, a fortune teller!" Ava licked the tips of her sugary fingers. "Come on, let's go in. I want to know if Derek's my tall, dark, handsome stranger or if there's another one waiting around the corner!"

A wooden board hung from a faded yellow and white striped tent, proclaiming that Madame Babushka was inside, waiting to reveal all in her crystal ball.

Ava peeped through a gap in the canvas. "Well, she certainly looks the part. Very wizened and mystical. Who's going in first?"

"I will." Betty deposited her candy floss stick in a nearby waste bin. "I could do with someone telling me if my love life's *ever* going to go further than making polite chit-chat." She grinned before sticking her head tentatively into the tent.

A gloom immediately descended upon her, the only light coming from a solitary candle on a rickety table at which Madame Babushka sat, a yellow silk scarf covering her hair and large hooped earrings dangling beside wrinkled cheeks.

With some effort, Betty tore her eyes away from the mesmerising swirling lights in the iridescent globe on the table and, when a sense of foreboding swept over her, she put it down to nothing more than her imagination and the murkiness of the tent.

Madame Babushka motioned to her, gesturing that she should sit in the chair opposite.

"That'll be a shilling, please, my dear." She slid a metal cup across the table, into which Betty dropped a silver coin.

The old woman ran her hands over the crystal ball and focused on its glassy depths. As minutes passed without any prediction issuing from her lips, Betty stifled a yawn and peered through the gloom at her watch.

"You shouldn't be in such a rush to find out your destiny, young lady," snapped Madame Babushka. "You could end up regretting your haste."

"What's that supposed to mean? And I haven't got all day, you know. I've been sitting here for..."

"Sssshhh!" The ancient clairvoyant pointed a gnarled finger. "You have an admirer. I foresee that his love for you will run deep for many years." She peered into the globe again and the candlelight cast mournful shadows on her face. "But your connection to him will put you in grave danger. Take heed of my prediction... Madame Babushka is never wrong."

Betty nodded. "Hmmm, I see, very interesting. Is there anything else?"

The old woman peered into the ball for a while longer before sinking back in her chair. "No. That's all. Madam Babushka has seen all there is to see."

Betty pushed herself up from the chair and flashed the woman a smile. *Nutty as a fruitcake.* "Okay. Thank you. I'll be off, then. Bye."

Ava and Harriett pounced on her. "Well? What did she say? Is Patrick Jones going to be the love of your life?"

Betty rolled her eyes. "I've never heard such a load of old codswallop! She said I have an admirer who's going to love me forever but that my connection to him will put my life in grave danger. What utter tosh. Mind you, nice work if you can get it. She charged me a shilling for that!"

"A shilling?! That's daylight robbery! Well, I'm not going in for that price, are you, Harriett?"

"Certainly not. I can think of far better things to do with my money. Like a ride on the big wheel, for one."

As they walked off, chattering nineteen to the dozen, Betty kept the uneasy feeling that had started to flutter in the pit of her stomach to herself

CHAPTER ONE
Sixty Years Later.

"For heaven's sake, Leo! Will you *please* watch what you're doing? You almost took my eye out with that chisel."

Harriett Reeves dodged the offending implement and put down a tray holding two cups and a plate of jam doughnuts.

"Sorry, love. It didn't occur to me that it wasn't a good idea to scratch the back of my head while it was still in my hand." Leo Reeves pecked his wife on the cheek and, placing his hands in the small of his back, stretched his aching muscles. "Come on, Harry. Tea's up."

"Oooh, aaah... I'm too old for this sort of thing." Harry Jenkins grumbled as he heaved himself up from the floor, his joints creaking in accompaniment. "Why did I ever agree to help you lay this blasted carpet?"

"Because you're a good friend, that's why." Harriett drummed her fingers on her hip as she reviewed the progress so far. "Hmmm. Yes, I think it's going to look very nice when you've finished—it'll be a good morning's work."

"Hmpf, it's all very well for you to say that. You haven't been crawling around on all fours for hours. Ooohhhh, aaaaah, my poor knees! I shall be ready for a hot bath and my bed tonight, make no mistake."

Harry eased himself into a chair and helped himself to a doughnut.

Ignoring him, Harriett walked across the bare, wooden floorboards. "You know, Leo, it's a shame these aren't in better condition. They'd look wonderful sanded and varnished with a couple of those big rugs we like. Mind you, I think... Oh, dear, what's this?" She pressed on an uneven board with the toe of her shoe and one end raised up towards her. "Well, we can't leave this board loose like this. You'll have to secure it before you lay the carpet over it. It looks like it isn't fixed at all."

"Will do, love. Give us five minutes and we'll get back to it." Leo wrapped his hands around his mug of tea and relaxed back in the chair.

"Don't leave it too long, will you? That was the whole point of starting early, remember? So you could get the job done before it got too hot. It's almost ten o'clock and it's awfully warm already." She glanced at her watch. "Anyway, I'll be leaving you in peace shortly—I'm meeting Ava and Betty for coffee. With any luck, my absence will help to hasten things along."

"Slave driver," mumbled Harry, as Harriett left the room, and he took another doughnut.

"I heard that, Harry Jenkins," she called over her shoulder.

"I might as well take a look at this now." Leo flexed his fingers. "Then we can get on—the sooner we get this finished, the better." He adjusted his kneepads and examined the loose floorboard. "Funny how we've been here for almost four years and never noticed it before."

"Well, it's close to the skirting board, that's why. You never walk over there, do you?" Harry handed over the hammer and a box of nails. "And if it hadn't been for old eagle-eyes, we'd probably have laid the new carpet right over the top."

Leo chuckled. "She doesn't miss much, I'll give her that. I remember once when... Oh, hang on, it looks like there's something underneath these boards." He reached into the floor space and pulled out a large tin, its colours still vivid despite the years that had passed since it had been filled with biscuits.

"What's inside?" Harry approached with caution.

"Dunno till I open it, do I?" Leo lifted the lid to reveal a bundle of envelopes, tied with string, on top of which lay a faded black and white photograph of a young, woman paddling in the sea—a pair of shoes in one hand, her skirt pulled up above her knees with the other. Her blonde hair was held back by an Alice band and she was looking out to sea, seemingly oblivious to the camera being trained on her.

"Who's that then?" Harry peered over Leo's shoulder. "Do we know her? She looks familiar?"

Leo nodded. "She should do. It's Betty."

ooooooo

Harriett flipped through the envelopes. "They're all addressed to Betty at her family home. According to the postmarks, they're sixty years old."

"They've all got 'Return to Sender' written on them. Did you see?" said Leo. "She obviously didn't want them."

"Well, we'll have to give them to her now," said Harriett, turning over an envelope.

"Who're they from?" asked Harry.

Harriett peered down her nose at the envelope she held at arm's length. "The return address is for a Mr. P. Jones. Hmmm, Jones. Who could that be, I wonder?"

"Yooo-hoooo! Only me!" Ava Whittington's shrill call pierced the reflective silence. "Morning, dears. You know, I was just speaking to that chap who lives in the bungalow across the road from Betty—you know, the one who always looks like he's wearing someone else's teeth? Anyway, he was telling me that when he went for his stroll this morning, there were two fire engines and a police car blocking off the entrance to the marina to traffic *and* pedestrians so, before we make a wasted trip, we'd better call Charlotte to find out what on earth's going on." She took a small bottle of cologne from her handbag and upturned it onto a pristine handkerchief which she dabbed on the base of her neck.

"Morning, Ava. We've just had a bit of a surprise." Harriett opened the box again. "Leo found this lot under the floorboards. They're all addressed to Betty."

Ava lifted a brow. "Betty? Who are they from?"

"A Mr. P. Jones, according to the return address, but he definitely wasn't the chap who lived here before we moved in. The old chap who passed away, remember?"

Ava flapped her handkerchief in front of her face. "Just a minute. That man—the one who knew Betty from way back—you must know the one I mean, Harriett? The one who used to gaze at her with that ridiculous gooey look on his face. We thought they were going to get together for a while when they were teenagers but then it all fizzled out. Know the one I mean? He lived here at Sunny Days for a while, didn't he? Don't you recall Betty saying what a stir he caused with all the single ladies when he moved onto the complex? Oh, come on, you *must* remember! We used to tease her about fixing the two of them up?"

"Aah, yes, I do remember. He only lived here temporarily though, didn't he—while he was waiting for a smaller place to become available? And then, when he moved out, a married couple moved in. Now, what was his name?" Harriett tapped her chin.

"Wasn't it Peter?" said Ava.

"No. No, it was...Patrick! That's it, it's just come to me," said Harriet. "Patrick Jones."

Ava snapped her fingers. "You're right! Patrick Jones. He was a bit of a showman if I remember correctly. Used to keep the people at Sunny Days entertained with his stories, and his impersonations, and his singing, so Betty said. And then he left quite suddenly, didn't he?"

"Wonder why she sent the letters back?" said Leo.

Harriett shrugged. "No idea but I seem to recall that he was a lot keener on Betty than she was on him. If he came on too strong, that would have definitely put her off. I'm fairly certain that she only wanted to be friends but Patrick wanted a very different relationship. The last thing she would have wanted to do was lead him on so I suppose that's why she returned them—she wouldn't have felt comfortable keeping them. They must have meant a lot to him to have kept them for so long, even though they must have been a constant reminder that she didn't want him."

"And she never mentioned receiving them?" asked Harry.

"Never. I mean, Ava and I suspected that Patrick was carrying a torch for her long after our teens but we had no idea he was *this* besotted." Harriett tapped her fingernails against the lid of the tin. "There must be a hundred letters in here."

"Wonder why she never told us about them?" Ava took a powder compact from her bag and removed all traces of the beginnings of a shiny nose.

"No idea, but I suggest we take them over to her now." Harriett picked up the tin and tucked it under her arm. "Right, won't be long, you two. Don't do anything we wouldn't do!"

ooooooo

Betty Tubbs flicked through the envelopes before returning them to the tin and firmly closing the lid. "Well, I don't remember that photograph—I'm sure he must have taken it without me knowing. And I don't understand why on earth he didn't throw all these letters out. After all, *I* didn't write them, he did."

Ava gave her eyes a theatrical roll. "Because, my dear, he was *in love* with you when he wrote them. They must have had great sentimental value—even if you did send them all back. Why else would he keep them for all those years? Seems to me that he loved you for all that time."

"So romantic." Harriett sighed. "Unrequited love—the most tragic kind."

"Well, I had *no* idea he felt that way for so long." Betty's usually kind voice was uncharacteristically harsh. "I mean, I knew he was keen but I never for a minute thought he was *that* keen. I only opened the first letter he sent and when I saw it was pages and pages of him telling me how he hoped I'd reconsider going out with him, I sent it straight back. Not that that put him off, mind you. He kept writing for months afterwards, and I kept returning the letters."

"Why *did* you send them back?" asked Ava.

"You must remember how shy I was back then? I just decided that life would be far less complicated without a man in it, so I didn't think it was appropriate to keep them in case he thought I was encouraging him."

"Did he ever ask you why you'd returned them all?"

Betty nodded. "Eventually. He saw me in town and took me to task about them. I had to get really cross with him before the message finally sunk in that I wanted him to stop writing to me. I told him that if he didn't, I'd never speak to him again. It all got a bit strained after that but at least it made it easier to avoid each other. We eventually lost touch completely and we didn't see, or speak to, each other again until he arrived at the retirement complex. We got quite friendly again, then, but everyone thought he had a soft spot for Nora Tweedie. When he was here, they were always going off for walks and out for afternoon tea. That's the sort of man he was, see? Always very giving of his time and the most wonderful company—it was such a shame when he left." She sighed and put the tin in a kitchen cupboard. "He must have been gone about four years now—time flies. Anyway, he certainly didn't give any indication that he still had feelings for me when he was here."

"Well, take it from me, no man keeps someone's photograph, and letters they wrote to them, for all this time unless he's pretty keen," said Ava. "What a pity he never told you. Who knows what might have happened?"

Betty sighed. "Hmm, who knows, indeed, but it's a bit late for that now. Right, that's enough reminiscing. Let's go and get some fresh air and a cup of coffee. I need to clear my head."

Ava delved in her bag for her phone. "I'm not sure we'll be able to go to Charlotte's Plaice—the marina's been closed off, apparently. I'll call Charlotte to see what's going on."

ooooooo

"No, Ava, we don't know what's happening yet but I think we might have to close the café for a while.

We can't go back there yet so we're killing time for an hour in The Fisherman's Rest. Okay, see you in a bit."

Having been evacuated from the marina while a team of engineers investigated the source of a gas leak, Charlotte Costello and best friend and co-worker, Jess Beddington, sat in a window seat of the centuries-old market square tea shop.

"I don't know about you but I'm starting to get quite excited about the prospect of having some time off. We've never closed the café in the summer." Charlotte stirred her tea with a straw, the gentle sound of the ice cubes clattering against the glass reminiscent of wooden wind chimes.

"Well, seeing as this is the second gas leak there's been in the past few years, I certainly don't fancy going back to work until it's sorted out." A smile as wide as her eyes turned up the corners of Jess's mouth as the waitress delivered a tall, espresso milk shake to the table, scoops of coffee ice cream bobbing enticingly on its creamy surface.

"It's a shame to miss out on a week of summer trade, though. You know how busy we are during the holidays—especially in August." Charlotte's fringe fell over her eye and she swept it back with a distracted sweep of her hand. "Mind you, it'll be worth it to be able to spend some more time with Molly. *And* it'll give Laura and Ava a break."

Charlotte's six-year old daughter, Molly, was well looked after by Charlotte's godmother, Laura, and Ava, who took turns to take care of her whenever Charlotte was at work. It was an arrangement that had been in place since she was born and it suited everyone.

Only half-listening, Jess pushed a long spoon down to the pool of thick, chocolate- mocha sauce at the bottom of her glass. "Yeah, I suppose."

A bell above the door tinkled, signalling the arrival of Charlotte's oldest friends.

"Helloooo, dears! We're here, at last."

Followed by wafts of lily of the valley, citrus and lavender, Ava, Harriett and Betty slumped into three chairs at a table under a whirring ceiling fan.

"Good heavens! This weather takes me back to when I was a girl." Ava dabbed her neck with her handkerchief. "We always used to have the most wonderful, long summers in those days. Not like now when you miss the entire season if you blink too many times." She flagged down a passing waitress. "Three white coffees, please, dear. And do you think you could turn up the fan? It's barely moving the air. Thanks muchly."

"Morning, ladies." Charlotte shuffled over to make room for them at the table. "Come on, come and sit over here—there's a bit of a breeze coming through the window."

"I didn't think we'd see you until your carpet had been fitted, Harriett," said Jess. "I thought you'd be overseeing the proceedings. Surely they haven't finished already?"

"No, they're still at it." Harriett fanned her glowing face with a menu. "Although I think they were quite pleased when I left them to it. They've had enough interruptions already this morning."

"Oh, yes, we *must* tell you!" said Ava gleefully. "Leo made quite a find under the floorboards. He…" She stopped mid-sentence as Betty cut her dead with a glare. "What? What have I done now? I didn't know it was a secret, Bet. You never said."

Betty shook her head. "It's *not* a secret but I've only just found out myself and I'm not sure how I feel about it yet so it would have been nice to have had a little time to mull it over before you broadcast it to the rest of St. Eves."

Charlotte and Jess exchanged a glance. "Only just found out about what?"

Betty blew out a sigh. "Oh well, I don't suppose it'll matter if you two know, but I'll let the girls tell you. I feel a bit embarrassed talking about it."

Harriett leaned across the table. "Leo found a biscuit tin under the floorboards. Full of old letters, it was. Love letters, no less. Addressed to Betty."

"All tied up in a bundle with a picture of her when she was a teenager," added Ava. "Isn't that the sweetest thing?"

"Who are they from?"

"Patrick Jones. He lived in the bungalow for a while some years back," said Harriett. "And it seems he was rather taken with our Betty."

"Really? Do we know him?" asked Charlotte.

"Um...well, kind of." Betty's cheeks flushed. "He came to Charlotte's Plaice a few times. You may remember once when he'd cut his foot on a broken shell after a crowd of us had been to the beach. You gave him some antiseptic and a plaster."

Jess squinted. "Was he quite tall? With a limp? Was that him?"

Betty nodded. "That's right, that was Patrick. One of his legs is a bit shorter than the other. Some condition passed on from his father."

"In that case, yes, I do remember. Didn't he leave his walking stick behind? It was black and gold, wasn't it? Very smart. And you came back for it."

Betty chuckled. "He forgot it because Nora and I were making such a fuss of him because of his foot. She had him by one arm and I had him by the other.

But yes, I did come back for it and you've got an excellent memory, Jess. It had a brass handle and brass fittings. Nora and I used to say to him, "Patrick, your walking stick's got more brass on it than a front door."

"Well, you don't look very happy about the letters being found." Jess winced and massaged away the brain freeze that shot to the bridge of her nose.

"Hmmm, well, it's stirred up some old memories. Memories I'd rather forget, if I'm honest."

"What memories?" Ava took a battery operated fan from her handbag and pointed it down the front of her blouse.

"You'll think I'm being silly," said Betty with a sheepish grin.

"No we won't," said Charlotte. "Something's obviously bothering you—what is it?"

Betty fiddled with her earring and shot a decidedly uncomfortable look at Ava and Harriett. "D'you remember that fortune teller I saw at one of the summer fairs when we were young? The one who told me I had a secret admirer—do you remember?"

"Hmmm, vaguely," said Harriett.

Ava's brows drew together. "Actually, I *do* remember her. Wrinkled little thing with a headscarf, wasn't she? Very mystical."

Betty nodded. "That's the one."

"What about her?" asked Charlotte.

"Well." Betty scratched her nose and cleared her throat. "She told me that my connection to an admirer would put me in danger. I worried about it for years but, when nothing happened, I put it out of my mind.

"Then Patrick turned up at Sunny Days and I started thinking about it again but, as nothing terrible happened and I thought he was keen on Nora, I forgot about it again after he left. But now these letters have been found and I'm all unsettled again.

"You'll think I'm silly, I know, but I've always been superstitious and, as I've never had another admirer—not that I'm aware of, anyway—I assume the fortune teller must have been referring to Patrick. And those letters are a connection to him, aren't they?"

"Oh, for heaven's sake, Bet!" Harriett was incredulous. "I can't *believe* you've been worrying about a ridiculous prediction that was made over half a century ago. And, if you have, why on earth have you never told us before now?" Her menu wafting became more vigorous.

"Exactly. What are friends for? You know, it's a disgrace that people are allowed to tell you things that can scare you half to death, and then charge you for the privilege. It shouldn't be allowed." Ava scowled and turned her fan up to high speed.

Doughnuts, Diamonds and Dead Men

"Well, I think it's lovely that he kept all the letters, Betty, and your photo." Charlotte patted her hand. "And I can see why you were concerned but, I have to agree, I think you're worrying unnecessarily. I mean, I don't see how any connection you had to this man is going to cause you problems now, particularly as he's not even *at* Sunny Days any more."

"I second that," said Jess, "and I'm pretty sure if danger was heading your way sixty years ago, it would have caught up with you by now. Honestly, what a load of old bunkum." She tipped up her glass for the very last drops of rich coffee goodness. "So, you're not in touch with him at all?"

Betty shook her head. "I don't even know where he went, although he often talked about wanting to spend his last years in the countryside. He was a real country boy, see. There wasn't a flower, tree, animal, bird, fish or insect that he didn't know about. His family came to St. Eves when he was eighteen but he lived in Somerset before then. A village called Sutton's Folly, if I remember. He used to joke with Nora and me that he was going to buy a country retreat and be Lord of the Manor and take us with him as his concubines."

"Doesn't anyone else know where he is? None of the other residents?"

"No. We all took turns trying his phone for a couple of days after he left but he never answered. We assumed that, because he'd left so suddenly, he didn't want to be found. He always used to say that he hated goodbyes so we guessed that was why he just vanished the way he did." Betty sipped her coffee. "We asked Cooper and Ellen if they knew where he'd gone but they were as surprised as we were when he cleared off."

"Cooper and Ellen?"

"Oh, they're the couple who manage the retirement complex."

"Apart from the letters, did he leave anything else behind?" asked Charlotte.

"Only the furniture," said Betty. "Actually, I remember Cooper being very cross about that—he had to pay someone to move it out. Patrick really should have cleared out everything from the bungalow before he left but the only things he took with him were his clothes and some personal things."

"Wasn't it him who gave you that ghastly painting? That pink and purple abstract abomination that's hanging above your fireplace?" said Ava.

"It's *not* an abomination! But yes, it was him. He gave it to me the night before he left. I'd popped round to see him and it was on the couch. It caught my eye straight away because I loved the colours and when I remarked on it, he immediately said that he wanted me to have it. To be honest, it sticks out like a sore thumb amongst my traditional country cottage décor but Patrick was so sweet. He walked me back to my place and put it on the wall for me and told me to think of him whenever I looked at it. I've grown awfully fond of it." She turned to Ava and jabbed her on the arm.

"And while I think of it, blabbermouth, if you should bump into Nora Tweedie, please don't say anything in front of her about Patrick leaving me the painting as a gift. She was very soft on him and I know it would put her nose out of joint to know he gave *me* something, but not her. It took her months to get over it when he left and I don't want to give her any reason to start wailing like a petulant toddler again."

"What I'd like to know is why he didn't take the letters with him when he moved out of Harriett's place," said Ava."

Charlotte signalled for the bill. "He probably had a lot on his mind with the move and he just forgot. And once he'd remembered, the new tenants would have settled in, wouldn't they? He could hardly go back and ask them if they'd mind moving their furniture and ripping up the carpet so he could get something he left under the floorboards."

Betty nodded. "Hmmm, I suppose you're right. And I suppose there was little point in him keeping them forever. They're just a bunch of his old, unwanted words, after all."

"What a shame you don't know where he is," said Jess. "You could send them on to him if you did. Then you wouldn't feel like you still had a connection to him."

"What a marvellous idea! Maybe we *can* send them to him, Bet?" said Ava. "If we could find out where he is."

"I already told you. I don't *know* where he is. And neither does anyone else."

"What about Nathan? Surely he could find out? Couldn't you ask him, Charlotte, dear?"

"Er, not really, Ava." Charlotte looked up from her purse as she hunted for some coins to leave for a tip. "He can't use the police computer to track someone down just because Betty wants to return a few old letters."

"Oh. What a bother." Ava returned her fan to the depths of her handbag. "I thought we'd cracked it, then."

"Never mind. It really doesn't matter." Betty hated to cause anyone any inconvenience. "I'll just keep them in a cupboard out of the way and try to forget about them."

Ava tutted. "You know what, Elizabeth Tubbs? You give up too easily. If we put our heads together, we'll track him down, you see if we don't." She inspected her reflection in the stainless-steel serviette holder and dabbed a powder puff over her nose. "Now then." She snapped the powder compact shut. "How about a spot of shopping before lunch?"

CHAPTER TWO

In the wake of a light lunch of perfect triangles of smoked salmon and cream cheese sandwiches, with the crusts neatly trimmed, followed by a generous slice of homemade strawberry cheesecake back at Betty's bungalow, Ava and Harriett relaxed in reclining armchairs in the comfort of the air-conditioned living room.

"Oh, this is bliss! Ava wiggled her toes and took a sip from a glass of homemade lemonade with just the right balance of sharp and sweet.

Harriett fumbled down the side of the chair for the TV remote and gave a sigh of contentment as she pressed a button and the opening credits for their favourite early-afternoon quiz show rolled up the screen.

"Has it started yet?" Betty appeared with a towel around her neck and a spinach and avocado concoction smeared liberally over her face.

"Only just. Mind you don't get any of that on your upholstery," said Harriett.

"I won't, that's what the towel's for." Betty settled down on the end of the couch and pulled a lever to raise the foot rest.

"Please tell me you're going to close the curtains while you're looking like the Jolly Green Giant's long-lost sister?" Ava's nostrils flared in horror. "You never know who might walk past and look in."

Unlike Betty, Ava was precious about who saw her when she wasn't looking her best.

Betty shook her head. "Ava, it's the middle of the afternoon and I've no intention of closing the curtains. Good grief, it's only a face mask. I couldn't care less if someone looks through the window and sees me like this. And if they don't like what they see, they shouldn't be so nosy, should they?" She reached for her lemonade. "Anyway, I've no intention of blocking out the sunlight. You know I like to keep my curtains open for as long as possible—I *never* close them until it's time to go to bed."

Once a week, the friends got together for a home-pampering session. Ava had given herself a manicure, Harriett had her feet in the foot-spa and Betty was trying a homemade facemask.

Ava gazed lazily out of the window, watching a car that came to a stop a little way down from the bungalow, outside the entrance to the retirement complex office. Its occupants spilled out and began unloading shopping bags from the boot.

"Is that the manager of the complex?" She peered over the top of her TV glasses.

Harriett pushed herself up on her elbow. "Yes, with his family."

"Thought so." Ava jumped up from the armchair and slipped her sandals on. "Won't be a minute."

"Where are you going? Ava? I hope you're not going to say anything about Patrick Jones. Ava...*Ava!*" Betty's cries went unheeded, the face mask preventing her from chasing after her loose-tongued friend.

"Yoooo-hoooo! Mr. er...Manager." Ava approached the car at a rapid pace, her heels click-clacking against the sultry tarmac.

A tall, blond man, his hair streaked with swathes of grey at his temples, turned and smiled causing the wrinkles at the outer corners of his grey-green eyes to curl upwards. "Are you talking to me?"

"Yes. I'm so sorry, dear. I don't know your name. I'm visiting some friends, you see."

The man held out his hand. "I'm Cooper Anderson and this is my wife, Ellen, our daughter, Jemima, and her husband, Gavin."

"Hello, all, very nice to meet you."

"What can I help you with?" Cooper kept one eye on Ava as he lifted a large box of groceries from the back of the car and placed it on a trolley.

"Well, I wanted to ask you about a gentleman who used to live here. He left rather suddenly and a friend of mine is trying to track him down. I wondered if you might have heard anything over the years about where he might be." Ava averted her gaze from Betty's bungalow, at which she could see a bright green face, and a shaking fist, at the window.

"Oh yes?" Cooper brushed beads of sweat from his brow. "And who might that be?"

"Patrick Jones. He lived in Leo and Harriett Reeves' place for a while until he moved to another property, so I understand."

The entire family stopped in their tracks, each head snapping round at the mention of Patrick.

Cooper straightened up. "Oh yes, we remember *him*...unfortunately. I had to pay out of my own pocket to have his place cleared out when he left and he didn't leave a forwarding address for us to send the bill to. I mean, it wasn't like he didn't have the money—he was loaded, by all accounts. If I ever see him again, I shall tell him *exactly* what I think of him."

"Oh, don't be like that Dad. He was a lovely old bloke." Jemima beamed. "I was really sad when he left. He was always so friendly and kind to me. I wish he was still here."

Gavin Campbell glared at his wife from beneath the flip-up lenses of his sunglasses, his jaw clenched, his face red and bloated from years of steroid use.

"What is the *matter* with you, Jem? Telling complete strangers how upset you were when some old guy you barely knew moved on. You know how that makes you sound? It makes you sound like someone who has an unhealthy obsession with old men, that's what."

A pair of faded khaki shorts hugged his huge thighs and the thin fabric of his white t-shirt strained across his chest as he heaved a sack of onions onto his broad shoulder. He gave his wife one last scowl before pushing past her and striding off to the kitchen, his footsteps heavy in a pair of well-worn, military issue combat boots.

Jemima stuck out her bottom lip and turned her head.

"Take no notice of him, love. He doesn't mean it." Ellen Anderson patted her daughter's arm in a motherly fashion. "He's under a lot of stress," she explained to Ava. "He's not usually as grumpy as that—we wouldn't adore him as much as we do if he was!" She hooted raucously.

Ava cast a glance at Cooper. *I'm not sure **he** feels quite the same way*, she thought as she followed his glare after his son-in-law.

"Anyway, Coop," said Ellen. "Wasn't Patrick always saying that he wanted to go and live in the countryside? *Cooper!*"

"What? Oh, sorry, um, yes, he was. He was always talking about it." Cooper tore his gaze away from Gavin. "But I've no idea where he went. Why do want to track him down, anyway, Mrs…?"

"Oh, my goodness, where are my manners." Ava blew on her fingernails and touched them to her cheek before holding out her hand. "Just checking my manicure's dry. Mrs. Ava Whittington. Very happy to make your acquaintance. We're trying to trace him to return something of his that was found in Mr. and Mrs. Reeves' bungalow."

"Really? Wherever did you find it?" Ellen picked up two shopping bags and promptly put them down again. "We would have checked everything when Patrick moved to the other bungalow to make sure nothing had been left behind." She leaned against the car and gathered her mousy hair from around her glowing face, securing it in a messy topknot. "Excuse me, won't you?" she said, wafting the bottom of her skirt around her knees. "I'm not sure if I'm having a hot flush, or it's this weather—both, probably. Anyway, what is it you've found?"

"Oh, nothing that would be of any interest to anyone else," said Ava. "Just some old letters under the floorboards that he'd written to an old sweetheart—nothing very exciting."

Ellen put her hands over her heart. "Oh, how adorable! I do hope you manage to find him. I'm sorry we can't help you but good luck in your search."

Jemima reached for Ava's arm. "If you track him down, will you send him our love?"

"Er, don't speak for me, please," said Cooper. "If you'd like Mrs. Whittington to pass on *your* regards, that's up to you, but I don't want him to think *I'm* sending him anything at all." He forced a smile. "Well, if there's nothing else, we must be getting on."

Cooper Anderson gave Ava a curt nod before turning on his heel.

The conversation was definitely over.

ooooooo

"Ava Whittington, I could flipping well *throttle* you! I already *told* you they didn't know where Patrick was!"

The bits of Betty's face that weren't green were as red as a London bus. "I specifically asked you *not* to go out there and what do you do? The exact opposite. I could *scream*, honestly, I could. Now you've told them I'm trying to get in touch with Patrick, they'll be thinking that I sit at home every night like a lonely old spinster, desperate to find a man." She flopped down into the chair and drummed her fingers on her knees, a frown creasing the green pulp between her brows.

"Oh, come on, Bet. They won't think that, and I didn't mean any harm. I was only trying to help." Ava laid a placatory hand on her friend's arm. "I could see how worried you were and you've already admitted that you'd feel better if you could return those letters. Well, I thought that if Mr. Anderson had heard anything about where Patrick might be, and you could send the letters back to him, there wouldn't *be* a connection to him any more and you could stop worrying about being in mortal peril...or whatever ridiculous thing it was that that fortune teller told you. You see, there's always a method to my madness."

A smile fluttered on Betty's lips. "Oh, you make me so cross, sometimes, but how can I not forgive you?" She squeezed Ava's hand. "So, come on then, what did you find out?"

"Well, nothing about where Patrick is, unfortunately, although the Andersons also mentioned that he'd wanted to move to the countryside. Other than that, I didn't find out much at all. Apart from that the son-in-law has the most appalling manners and speaks to his wife like dirt. Mrs. Anderson tried to sweep it under the rug by making excuses for him but no man should speak to his wife like that. Poor thing— I felt terribly sorry for her."

"Erm, you didn't tell them *why* we wanted to find Patrick, did you?" Betty asked, warily.

"Yes, of course I did." Ava rolled her eyes. "Why? What have I done wrong now?"

"Oh dear," said Betty. "It's just that Ellen Anderson is a bigger blabbermouth than you, and this place is a gossipmonger's paradise. They thrive on gossip in the club house. Remember, some of them don't get out much so a bit of scandal brightens up the day for them."

"That's dreadful!" exclaimed Ava. "A manager should be the sole of discretion. I can't believe she'd repeat something a resident had told her in a private conversation."

"Hmpf, well, she does." Betty nodded, emphatically. "She can sniff out a juicy piece of gossip from miles away—she's like a bloodhound. As long as it's not about her, or her family, it's fair game as far as she's concerned."

"Well, if it's any consolation, she didn't seem that interested." Ava admired her freshly manicured nails. "She was far too preoccupied with her hot flushes and making excuses for her son-in-law."

Betty wrung her hands. "I hope you're right. I really would prefer that news of the letters doesn't get back to Nora Tweedie. We've become very friendly over the years, going to bingo and playing cards, but her nose will be well and truly put out of joint if she finds out that Patrick was fond of me, particularly as everyone thought he had a soft spot for *her*."

Ava flapped a dismissive hand. "Oh, Bet, stop fretting. They're just some old letters he wrote—they'll hardly even register on the gossip scale. And, anyway, now I think about it, I'm sure I didn't say who they were addressed to, just that they were found in

Harriett and Leo's bungalow. So you see? It's so uninteresting, I'm sure it won't even make it to the club house. Really, don't spend another second worrying about it."

ooooooo

Betty knew immediately that her worst fears had come to pass when she arrived at the club house that evening.

At a nearby table, Nora could barely contain her excitement, her round cheeks flushed and her eyes sparkling as she beckoned Betty to join her.

"Oh, thank goodness you're here! I've been bursting to tell you the news! Come on, I've saved you a seat. Come and sit down and I'll tell you all about it. You'll never *believe* what's happened!"

Betty glanced around the room. Even if she hadn't already known, it wouldn't have taken long for her to find out—the air was abuzz with the hum of chatter about the letters which had been found under the floorboards in bungalow number eleven.

Nora leaned forward and lowered her voice. "When Patrick Jones moved out of that bungalow, the one where your friends live now, he left some letters behind. *Love* letters, if you please."

"Erm, yes, I heard about it earlier." Betty fiddled with the collar of her blouse. "Gosh, it's stuffy in here, isn't it?"

Ignoring her, Nora continued. "You know what everyone's saying?"

Betty shook her head. "What?"

"That the letters were written to *me*, of course! Patrick must have been dying to give them to me but didn't have the nerve, poor thing. And then, when he moved out, they got left behind and one thing led to another, and under the floorboards is where they stayed. Can you believe it? All that time he was at Sunny Days, he really *was* in love with me!" Nora sighed and sent a beatific smile around the room.

"Anyway, I was wondering if you'd mind speaking to Harriett for me? To ask her for the letters, I mean. I *could* ask her myself but you know her better than I do. Between you and me, I think it's a bit off that she hasn't given them to me already. I mean, they're not hers to keep, are they?"

Betty's wooden smile would have looked perfectly at home on a ventriloquist's knee. This was exactly the scenario she'd wanted to avoid.

Nora gave her a knowing look and patted her hand. "Are you alright? You look awfully upset. Look, I know you were probably keen on him, too—so many of us were—but please, let's not fall out over this. We're not going to let a man ruin our friendship, are we?"

Betty knew she couldn't keep the secret. She couldn't let Nora carry on thinking the letters had been written to her, and she knew no good would come of holding back the truth, so she crossed her fingers and hoped for the best.

"Look, Nora, there's something I have to tell you. I didn't want you to find out because I know how fond of Patrick you were but, I'm sorry, he didn't write the letters to you."

The smile vanished from Nora's face. "Eh? What d'you mean? They must have been to me—who else would he have written them to?"

Betty hesitated. "To me," she said quietly. "He wrote them to me."

Nora stared for what seemed like an age. Then she hooked her handbag over the crook of her elbow, tossed her head, and made a beeline for the exit, looking neither left nor right, and ignoring calls from the other residents to join them at their tables for an in-depth chinwag.

Betty sighed deeply and followed suit.

ooooooo

The following morning, as she walked the short distance to Harriett's bungalow, Betty became aware of stares being thrown her way and comments being whispered behind furtively raised hands.

It wasn't until no one answered her good morning greetings, and Nora Tweedie passed by with Bea Berry and Jocelyn Pickler, two of the bitchiest women on the complex, all three of them making a point of very deliberately looking the other way, that Betty felt angry tears prick the backs of her eyes.

I don't believe it. They're ignoring me!

CHAPTER THREE

At Charlotte's Plaice café, Charlotte and Jess were preparing for an unexpected hiatus.

For the next week, at least, the marina was being closed off to allow for the repair of the recently discovered gas leak.

"Well, I don't know about you but I'm going to spend my time off getting up late and working on my tan." Jess peered at her pale reflection in the mirror and pulled a face "I look like I've been living underground for the past six months. What are you going to get up to?"

Charlotte shrugged. "No plans, but we won't be short of things to do. You know you're always welcome to spend some time with Molly and I, don't you?" She shook out a tablecloth and folded it neatly.

"Yeah, I'd like that."

Their conversation was interrupted by a familiar, high-pitched greeting.

"Yooo-hooo, girls, it's only us!"

Ava, Harriett and Betty appeared on the terrace from around the corner. "Oh, are you late opening? Where are all the tables and chairs?"

"We have to close, Ava," said Charlotte. "Because of that gas leak. We'll be closed for at least a week, maybe more. We're only here now because the engineers have given all the business owners a morning to come and do anything that needs doing before they start work; cancel deliveries, clear out the fridges, that sort of thing."

"Oh, I see." Ava put her hand on her hip. "Well, that's a bother. Where are we going to go for coffee every day?"

"Ava, we're not the *only* café in St. Eves. I'm sure you'll find somewhere to go for a week or two...if they'll put up with you for that long." Charlotte winked. "And you can always pop round to my place for a chat and a cuppa if you get withdrawal symptoms. Anyway, you can sit down inside if you want, while Jess and I finish up. Er, Betty, are you alright?"

Betty dabbed at her eyes behind her sunglasses and waved away Charlotte's concern. "Oh, don't take any notice of me, love, I'm just feeling a bit sorry for myself, that's all." She sniffed and blew her nose.

"Actually, if you must know, Charlotte, no, she's not alright," Harriett blurted. "Those *horrible* women at Sunny Days are completely ignoring her. Honestly, it makes my blood boil. You'd think people of their age would have a bit more sense between their ears."

"What? Why?"

"Because Nora Tweedie heard about the letters and when she found out Patrick had written them to

Betty, she got the raving hump. It's not Betty's fault, for goodness' sake. Honestly, I could throttle her."

"So, Nora thought Patrick had written the letters to *her*? And now she's not speaking to you?" Jess shook her head.

"Yes, she did. And no, she's not. And nor are half the other residents on the complex. Nora obviously didn't waste any time telling everyone what happened. She probably laid it on thick—telling everyone how I upset her—and now everyone's avoiding me." Betty puffed out a frustrated sigh. "Honestly, it's so ridiculous—it's not a contest. I mean, what is it they say? 'All's fair in love and war'? Well, it obviously isn't as far as Nora's concerned."

"I feel so responsible, Betty. I hope you know that the last thing I wanted was to cause you any upset," said Ava. "Honestly, if I could get close enough, I'd poke that flipping Nora Tweedie in the eye—no, make that *both* eyes. It's not your fault that Patrick Jones wasn't in love with her, for heaven's sake."

"I know you didn't mean any harm," said Betty. "It's those damn letters! They're already causing trouble. I wish I could get rid of them!"

"Why don't you just throw them out?" asked Jess.

"No, I couldn't. As much as I wish I'd never laid eyes on them, it wouldn't seem right to put them in the rubbish bin. No, I'll just keep them somewhere, out of sight."

"You know, I was thinking," said Jess. "Wouldn't Patrick have gone back to where he used to live before he came to St. Eves?" said Jess. "Sutton's Folly, you said, didn't you?"

"Yes, but I don't think he'd have gone back there. He never even used to want to talk about it. Every time we brought it up he changed the subject. I think it was because he'd been away from it for so many years, it's probably not somewhere he felt was home any more. No, I don't think that's where he went." Betty tapped her chin. "Although he could have changed his mind, I suppose. Oh dear, I don't know."

Charlotte took out her phone. A few taps later, she announced triumphantly, "According to this, there are two retirement homes, each less than half a mile away from Sutton's Folly; 'Hill View' and 'Forest Dell'. What do you think, Betty?"

"I don't know," said Betty cautiously. "I suppose I could call to find out if Patrick's staying at either of them."

"Would they give out that information over the phone?" said Harriett.

"Hmm, not sure," said Jess as she wiped down the window frames. "My gran was in a care home for a while after she had a fall and they wouldn't give us any information over the phone until we'd answered a whole list of security questions to prove we were family. If that's anything to go by, I doubt they'll tell you anything."

"Oh, well, not to worry." Betty put on a smile. "I never really expected to find an address for him, anyway. Like I said, I'll just put the letters away in a cupboard and forget about them."

"Or..." Charlotte muttered from behind the bar.

"You know talking to yourself's a sign of going bonkers, don't you?" Jess threw her a sideways glance.

"Or..." Charlotte repeated, "you could *totally* forget about locking Patrick's letters away in a cupboard, Betty, *or* sending them back to him. Why don't we *go* to Sutton's Folly? I've got to close the café, Molly's on holiday, Nathan will be okay on his own for a week and you look like you could do with getting away from Nora Tweedie for a few days. I'll see if we can get a late booking somewhere and we can pack up the car and be there in a few hours. What do you think?"

"Er, hello." Jess waved. "What about me? Don't think you're going on a road trip without me."

"Well, if you're going," said Ava, "we're coming, too. Harriett?"

Harriett shrugged. "Fine by me."

"Well, if we're all going, we'll need another driver."

Jess's hand shot up.

"Right, then." Charlotte grinned. "And I'll have to bring the dogs. I could never put them in kennels and it wouldn't be fair to ask Leo or Harry to look after them at such short notice. Ooh, and we could ask Laura, too. She's always going on about how we don't see enough of each other." She hugged herself and then remembered the reason for the suggestion in the first place. "But it's your decision, Betty. D'you fancy a break?"

Betty's frowned. "Well, I'm not sure Patrick would be terribly pleased if I tracked him down. What if he doesn't want to be found?" She chewed her lip. "But on the other hand, I *would* like to get shot of those letters."

She took a long look at the excited faces around her and clapped her hands. "Oh, why not? Sutton's Folly, here we come!"

ooooooo

"Mummy, are we nearly there yet?" Molly's sleepy voice drifted from the back seat of the car.

"That must be the hundredth time you've asked. Yes, sweetheart, not long now."

Having sat for an age in a queue of almost-stationary cars which snaked from one county to the next, Charlotte was relieved to be making up time at last. It appeared that everyone else had also thought that leaving before the sun came up would be the best time to travel, and they'd all got caught in the same traffic jam.

"How long do you think it *will* take, dear?" Ava peered over Charlotte's shoulder at her new hair-do in the interior mirror. She'd had the ends of her steel-grey bob tinted pastel pink especially for the trip and was admiring her new look at every opportunity. "My tummy's feeling a little gripey."

Charlotte caught Ava's eye in the mirror and raised a brow. "If we don't get caught up again, we should be there in about half an hour but we only stopped for a break forty minutes ago. Are you feeling alright? Do you want me to pull over?"

"Mummy, Ava smells nasty."

"*Molly!* Apologise at once, please! Honestly, what's got into you?" Charlotte mouthed an apology to Ava in the mirror. "So, anyway, *do* you want me to pull over?"

"No, no, I'm fine," Ava reassured. "And don't be too harsh on Molly, dear, she's probably right. I've been snacking on these since we left St. Eves and I think I've eaten a little too many. I bought a pound because the deli had it on special offer. They make their own on the premises, you know." She belched behind her hand and then leaned forward and shook a cardboard box under Charlotte's nose. "Breaded tripe, dear?"

Charlotte recoiled as the box came into her peripheral vision. "Oh my God, Ava! No thanks—really. I thought that smell was the dogs' chews."

"Suit yourself." Ava shrugged "You don't know what you're missing—it's so moreish, once you have one piece, you just can't stop."

"I'm pretty sure *I* could," mumbled Charlotte as, with a sigh of relief, she took the next exit and followed the signs to Sutton's Folly.

ooooooo

A chalet with pale, primrose-yellow painted walls and a Cornish slate roof gleamed in the late morning sunlight and, as the car came to a stop outside, Charlotte felt the stress of the long drive fall away.

Molly rubbed her eyes as she lifted her head from Ava's arm. "Are we there yet?"

"Yes, darling, we're here. Come on, jump out and you can stretch your legs while we unpack the cars and the dogs have a run around. I need an hour to take Betty somewhere, and then we'll find somewhere to have lunch. Okay?"

"'Kay, Mummy."

ooooooo

"This is exciting, isn't it?" Betty trained her eyes on the entrance to Hill View retirement complex from the passenger seat of Charlotte's car, the tin of letters on her lap. "It's like a take-out."

"You mean a stake-out." Charlotte giggled.

"Do I?" Betty shrugged a shoulder. "Whatever."

"You know, it says here that 'Hill View' used to be the principal residence of the Earl of Wussocks." Charlotte swiped the screen of her phone. "He sold it in 1997 to pay off family debts and it was converted to a retirement complex six years later."

"Hmmm, that doesn't surprise me." Betty cast her gaze over the grand, Georgian edifice. "Look at all those features—I'm sure they're original. You can tell by the... Oooh, look, there are some people just coming out of the gate. Come on!"

Charlotte scrambled to follow, catching up just as Betty called out to the couple ahead. "Hello...excuse me."

The man turned and a light breeze wafted his ginger comb-over upright, reminiscent of a rooster's crest.

"Yes?"

"I'm sorry to trouble you. I wonder if you could help me?" Betty beamed. "I'm looking for an old friend—Patrick Jones. You wouldn't happen to know him, would you? I was hoping we might find him here."

The man shook his head. "Can't help you, I'm afraid. He's definitely not a resident here. We'd know if he was—there are only fifteen private apartments on the complex and we know all the owners. Do you recognise the name, Daphne?"

His wife tilted her head and made a sympathetic cooing noise. "Nooo, I'm sorry. Like my husband said, we know everyone and that name doesn't ring a bell at all."

There was no need for Betty to say how much she'd been looking forward to seeing Patrick; her crestfallen face said more than words ever could have.

Charlotte put an arm around her shoulder. "Okay, thank you. You've been very helpful."

They walked back to the car in silence.

"We've still got one more place to look. Perhaps he'll be there," said Betty hopefully.

"I hope so," said Charlotte.

"I was convinced he'd be here, you know."

"I know you were." Charlotte squeezed Betty's hand as she turned the key in the ignition. "Come on, let's get back to the others. We'll have the smile back on your face in no time!"

ooooooo

"What a gorgeous old place."

Jess took a picture as they approached the small, country pub. At the end of a tree-lined lane, the tall boughs on either side stretched up and intertwined to create a covered walkway offering weary travellers some respite from the heat.

"It's like a fairy tale house, isn't it, Mummy?"

With three higgledy-piggledy chimneys standing proud of a neatly thatched roof, and warm, stone walls brought to life by weighty hanging baskets overspilling with brilliantly coloured Petunias, the pub could have, indeed, been taken straight from the pages of a fairy tale.

Wooden benches and tables with large sun umbrellas were welcome additions to the sprawling garden, as was a large shaded area with a vast bowl of water for thirsty dogs.

"Yes, sweetheart, it does. And it looks perfect. Come on, let's grab a table and then Jess and I will go inside for some drinks and get some lunch organised. I'm starving."

"Would you mind asking how long it'll take to get to Forest Dell?" asked Betty. "The sooner I can get rid of those letters, the sooner I can stop worrying and start enjoying myself."

"With Patrick Jones, you mean?" Ava gave her a nudge and a crafty wink.

"No, definitely *not*!" Betty's cheeks turned bright pink. "I *meant* I could start enjoying myself with you lot."

"Course I'll ask." Charlotte grinned. "And we'll bring some menus out."

"Just a tonic water for me, please," called Ava, looking decidedly green around the gills. "I couldn't face anything to eat just now."

The pub was busy with locals, all of whom turned from their positions at the bar when Charlotte and Jess walked in.

"What can I get you, ladies?" A stocky woman with a mullet and a face that told them she wouldn't tolerate any nonsense extended a tepid welcome with the briefest of smiles.

"Three shandies, two lemonades, a tonic water and a bottle of water, please. And some menus. Oh, and a big bottle of water, too."

"Who's that for?" asked Jess.

"It's to pour over the dogs. To cool them down a bit."

At the mention of dogs, the woman's expression changed completely, her smile reaching all the way up to her eyes. "You've got dogs? What are they?"

"A West Highland Terrier and a Heinz 57."

The woman reached under the bar and passed two bone-shaped dog biscuits to Charlotte. "'Ere, on the 'ouse. I'm a sucker for dogs, I am."

"Thank you, that's kind." Encouraged by the woman's slight thaw, Charlotte pressed for information.

"Forest Dell? Yeah, it's on the edge of the village, 'bout fifteen minutes from 'ere." The woman jerked her thumb over her shoulder as she topped up a glass with beer. "You visitin' someone?"

"Not exactly. We're looking for a friend of a friend. He used to live around here years ago."

"Oh? What's 'is name? I know most people and a lot of folk from the retirement 'ome come in for Sunday lunch."

"Patrick Jones."

The woman shook her head. "Never 'eard of 'im. 'E must be a new arrival."

"Actually, we think he might have been at the home for about four years, maybe a bit less," said Jess.

The woman shook her head even more vehemently. "Well, I'm tellin' you, he definitely 'ain't at Forest Dell. I'd know the name if 'e was 'cos I never forget a name, do I Bill?"

A dishevelled young patron with wind-chapped cheeks, and lips to match, pushed up the peak of his flat cap with an index finger and shook his head. "She don't forget nothin'. Got a memory like an elephant with a grudge, that one."

"And if 'e used to live 'ere, it must 'ave been before my time 'cos I'd know 'im otherwise," the woman continued. "The Sutton's Folly Mafia might know 'im, though."

Charlotte and Jess exchanged a glance.

The woman grinned and nodded to a table in the corner at which four elderly men were engrossed in a game of dominoes. "'Ere, Bert. You got a minute to 'ave a word with these ladies? They're lookin' for someone you might know."

A heavy-set man turned, his clear, grey eyes curious in his weathered face.

"Oh yes. And who might that be, then?" He spoke with a raspy eloquence, each word clearly enunciated despite the unlit pipe clamped firmly between his teeth.

"Patrick Jones. He lived here about sixty years ago—probably more."

Bert's pint of beer stilled mid-way to his mouth. He removed the pipe and glanced at his companions.

"You mean Flo and Henry's son?"

Charlotte shook her head. "I'm sorry, I don't know his parents' names. Only that they used to live here. Do you know him?"

Bert rested a foot on the rail of a nearby chair. "I should say I do. We *all* know him. Never thought

we'd hear the name around here again, though. Not
after what happened."

Charlotte stole a glance at Jess and took a step
forward. "Oh? And what *did* happen?"

Bert nudged the chair away from him with the
toe of his canvas espadrille and pulled another one
from a nearby table. "Come and sit down, and I'll tell
you."

ooooooo

"Patrick had an older sister. Lucy, her name
was. He adored her. We all did, come to that—she was
gorgeous. In fact, you courted her for a while, didn't
you, Finlay?" Bert addressed a man at the table who
acknowledged the question with a nod.

"I did. Until Fred Bainbridge come along with 'is
sharp suits and fancy car and stole 'er away from me.
She fell for 'im, 'ook, line and sinker. I never stood a
chance." He scowled as he recalled the memory.

"Anyhow," continued Bert, "before we knew it,
Lucy and Fred were engaged. And that's when all the
trouble started."

"What trouble?"

"The arguments and the fights. He loved her too
much, he used to say. So much that he couldn't bear
for her to be out of his sight. He became very
possessive—started following her everywhere to check
she really was where she said she would be, and with

whom. She was flattered to begin with but things got out of hand very quickly. She insisted that she wasn't seeing anyone else but he didn't believe her."

"And that's when 'e started gettin' a little *too* possessive." Finlay's clenched knuckles whitened.

"What d'you mean?" Jess frowned.

"Well, we're not sure that he ever hit her but he certainly pushed her around." Bert placed a domino and took a sip of his pint. "They were walking home one evening after booking The Kings Arms for their wedding reception and they got into an argument. According to eyewitnesses, there were raised voices and then he shoved her. She stumbled and the bus driver couldn't stop in time. She fell right in front of him."

"Oh no, that's awful!" Charlotte's hand flew to her mouth. "I take it the outcome wasn't good?"

Bert shook his head. "No, she died there and then. Fred was beside himself but he wouldn't take responsibility for the accident."

"And what happened after that?" asked Jess.

"Well, first thing that happened was that Patrick beat the living daylights out of Fred when he heard the news. It's a wonder he wasn't arrested himself," said Bert.

"Yeah, 'e might 'ave been six inches shorter and five years younger than Bainbridge but, by God, 'e

taught 'im a lesson." Finlay noted the surprised
expressions from Charlotte and Jess. "Your faces look
like ours did when we saw the state of Bainbridge's
face after Patrick 'ad finished with 'im. 'E'd never said
boo to a goose before then so we was surprised to find
out 'e was as strong as an ox. Bit wobbly at times,
mind you, on account of 'is leg, but that didn't stop 'im
makin' mincemeat of Bainbridge."

"Anyhow, long story short," continued Bert,
"Fred eventually got fifteen years. That day in the
courtroom—I remember it like it was yesterday—he
was furious that the jury found him guilty. And he was
furious with Patrick. He used to be a good-looking
bloke until Patrick rearranged his face—he'd grown
accustomed to his nose being in the middle of it, see?
He kicked and screamed when he was led down to the
cells—swore to Patrick that he'd hunt him down when
he got out and pay him back. Said he was going to
destroy everything he'd ever loved, no matter how long
it took."

"So, is that when Patrick left Sutton's Folly?
After Fred was sent to prison?"

Bert nodded. "Not just Patrick, his parents, too.
None of them wanted to stay here after what
happened to Lucy. I know it broke their hearts to
leave, though. They all loved it here." He jabbed at the

air with the empty pipe. "You say you think he might have come back here?"

Charlotte shrugged a shoulder. "I don't know. Our friend thinks so but it sounds like someone here would know if he had."

"I should think we would," agreed Bert. "Being such a small village, most people know most people. I'm certain if he'd come back here, we'd have heard about it from someone by now." He put the pipe back between his teeth and returned to his game of dominoes. "I have a feeling your friend's going to be disappointed."

Charlotte and Jess nodded as they stood up to leave. "Thanks for your help. We still don't know where Patrick is but at least we know where he isn't," said Charlotte.

"Come on." Jess pulled on Charlotte's sleeve. "We've been ages—they'll be dying of thirst out there."

The barmaid pushed the tray of drinks across the bar. "If you're still 'ere next Sunday, it's our annual fun-day. You can't miss it—it'll be on the village green—and there's always loads to do for the kiddies *and* the adults. It'll be too hot for the dogs, though."

"Okay, thanks for the tip. We'll be sure to stop by."

Doughnuts, Diamonds and Dead Men

As they carried the drinks outside, Jess whispered, "Sounds like Patrick isn't here after all. This place is even smaller than St. Eves so I'm pretty sure word would have got out if he'd come back. Like that guy said, most people know most people."

"Hmmm, I still think it's worth checking at the other home. We're already here, after all, so we might as well."

"I bet Betty doesn't know anything about what happened to Patrick's sister. I'm sure she'd have said if she did."

"We'd better break the news gently, then." Charlotte fixed a smile on her face and put down the tray she was carrying.

"Good grief! What took so long?" said Ava, clutching her throat. "I feel like I'm swallowing sand."

"Well? Did you find out anything?" Betty spoke before Charlotte could even open her mouth.

"Yes. The woman in the pub said that 'Forest Dell' isn't far from here. I'll drive you there later. For now, though, let's order some food!"

CHAPTER FOUR

A fruitless visit to Forest Dell retirement home, followed by learning of Patrick's sister's untimely demise, had put Betty well and truly in the doldrums.

"Look, I'm sorry to be a party pooper," she'd said, when valiant attempts to bring a smile back to her face had failed miserably. "Just get on with your holiday and don't mind me. I just need to think about things for a while."

"You're not still worried about what that fortune teller said, are you?" Jess had asked.

"Well, I won't lie, I'd feel happier if I'd been able to give the letters back to Patrick but I couldn't, and that's that." Betty had been pragmatic. "Just give me a while and I'll be alright. I just need to be alone with my thoughts for a bit."

Out of earshot, the friends had whispered their concerns but, by Sunday, good company and Molly's antics had cheered Betty up considerably.

As they got ready for the fun-day, their loud chatter competed with the inane musings of a radio DJ who seemed convinced that listeners would rather listen to him than music.

"Are we taking the dogs, Mummy?"

"No, sweetheart. It'll be too hot for them. They'll be better off here in the dog run. They've got plenty of water, plenty of room to run around and it's all in shade. They love it out there and we'll be back before they know it."

Molly squashed her nose up against the glass of the door to see Pippin and Panda stretched out on the grass, enjoying a snooze. Happy that they were in the best place, she nodded. "'Kay."

"Right, everyone ready? Let's get going, then!"

ooooooo

Molly slid her hand into Charlotte's, her eyes popping as they followed a young boy who had just finished being transformed into a frighteningly realistic zombie. "Mummy, look! Can I have my face painted? Pleeease?"

Charlotte eyed the little boy's gory makeup reluctantly. "Not like that, surely, Mol?"

"No!" Molly giggled. "Like a fairy princess, of course."

"Oh, okay. Come on then, let's go and have a chat with the lady and see what she can do. See you all soon—I'm sure we won't be too long. We'll find you later."

"I'll come, too." Laura took Molly's other's hand and she and Charlotte swung her all the way to the face-painting stall.

"Okay, dears, see you soon." Ava called after them and delved in her handbag to produce her powder puff which she pressed against her nose. "If this heat doesn't finish me off first," she mumbled, under her breath.

"Oh, stop being such a moaning Minnie." Betty tucked her arm through Ava's. "Come on, there's a refreshments kiosk over there. Let's go and get an ice cream and have a sit down. My feet could do with a rest. Harriett, Jess, you fancy an ice cream?"

Harriett and Jess had their heads together, talking quietly.

"*Harriett!*"

Harriett spun round. "What? Sorry, we were just looking at that tent over there."

"What tent?" Betty craned her neck.

"Er, that one down there. It's a fortune teller," said Jess.

"Hmpf, I'll be sure to steer clear of it, then." Betty turned back to the refreshments kiosk.

"Well, actually, we were just saying what a good idea we think it would be if you went in and had another reading." Harriett looked hopeful. "Hearing a different one would help you move on, don't you think?"

"Exactly." Jess took up the cause. "Because then you can forget about that absurd premonition from sixty years ago and get on with your life. You'll feel so much better afterwards—I know you will."

"You know, that's not a bad idea," agreed Ava. "In fact, I think it's splendid! What d'you think, Bet?"

Betty stared at the tent. A hand-written blackboard outside announced, in large, white, chalk lettering, that 'Cato DeLyon, Fortune Teller of the past, present and future', could be found beyond the scarlet and white canvas with the invitation to 'Step this way for Palm, Tea leaves, Astrology and Tarot Readings '.

"Well?" Ava tapped her foot expectantly.

'Betty's expression was pensive. "Hmmm, I could, I suppose. It *would* be nice to have a fresh start—not to have to think about it any more."

"Our point exactly!" Harriett grabbed her by the arm. "Come on, let's get it over with—the sooner the better." She marched her down to the tent and they waited outside.

A middle-aged woman with wild hair had her ear pressed against the canvas door flap, on which there was a sign that read, 'Reading in progress'. She put a finger to her lips.

"It's okay," she whispered. "My sister's in there. She won't mind me listening. She wants to know if she's going to get together with the chap she met at her pottery evening class. She's fancied him for months. Her decree absolute came through last week, y'see, and she's been like a cat on hot bricks ever since."

She leaned towards Betty. "Between you and me, I don't know how she stayed with her husband so long—twenty-eight years they were together and, in all that time, they barely spoke two words to each other." Perplexed, she shook her head. "Anyway, she's dying to move on with her life and as soon as she saw the board, she said, "Deirdre, I'm going in." He's supposed to be very good, y'know."

"You see, Betty," scolded Ava, "if you'd only confided in us before, we could have done this years ago,"

The door flap opened and a woman with equally wild hair appeared, fanning her pink face with a folded magazine.

"Well?" demanded her sister. "Was he any good?"

"Oh, Deirdre, he was fabulous—*so* accurate! He read my palm. Told me that a long-term relationship had recently come to an end and I should expect to meet the man of my dreams in the very near future. It's remarkable how they know these things, isn't it?"

Betty raised a doubting eyebrow but said nothing to quash the woman's high spirits. Instead, she gave her a benign smile and waited until she'd gone on her way before turning on her heel.

Doughnuts, Diamonds and Dead Men

"Oi, where d'you think you're going?" Harriett caught her by the sleeve.

"Oh, come on! Did you hear what she said? And did you see the indentation on her wedding ring finger? It must have been half an inch deep! It's no wonder that Cato the Conman knew she'd recently come out of a long-term relationship. It doesn't need a lot of mystical powers to deduce that she's worn a ring on that finger for years. And, honestly, telling her she's going to meet the man of her dreams...really? The man of her dreams, my foot. That must be the oldest line in the book—I can't believe fortune tellers are still using it."

"Oh dear, I suppose you're right," said Harriett, decidedly deflated.

"What a shame," said Ava. "I was rather hoping this was the opportunity for you to put all your concerns behind you."

"Yes, it would have been good, wouldn't it?" said Jess. "To not have to worry about that stupid prediction for the first time in years."

Betty looked from one friend to the other. She knew they only had her best interests at heart and she was touched by their concern so she put on a smile and turned back to the tent.

"I can tell I'm going to get no peace from you three until I give in, am I? Alright then, I'll go in but if he starts spouting nonsense about tall, dark, handsome strangers, large inheritances, or any such similar rubbish, I'm walking out, so don't be surprised if I'm not in there for very long, will you?" She chuckled and poked her head through the door flap. "Anyone home?"

A deep voice issued from inside the tent. "Please, come in. You're most welcome at Cato's table."

Betty pulled back the door flap to reveal Cato DeLyon. A young, slight man with pale hair, poker-straight and flowing past his shoulders, sat behind a large table, his watery, green eyes magnified through wire-rimmed glasses. He smiled at the others as they peered in, curious to see the enigmatic Cato DeLyon for themselves.

"When you're ready, Madam, would you pull the flap closed behind you, please?"

Outside, Ava, Harriett and Jess breathed a sigh of relief.

"I do hope he manages to put her mind at rest," said Harriett.

"Well, he should do. He only looks about twelve," replied Ava. "Not at all the imposing figure I expected, which is just what Bet needs to put her at ease. Much better than one of those witch-like old dears peering into a crystal ball from underneath a dodgy headscarf."

"I agree. I'm so glad she decided to see him," said Harriett. "I really think it'll do her the world of good." She took a floppy sunhat from her bag and pulled it down over her forehead.

"Quite," said Ava. "I mean, it's psychological, isn't it? She just needs something to help change her train of thought and she'll feel like a weight's been lifted off her shoulders."

"Oh, look, here they come." Jess held out her arms as Molly ran down the slight incline towards them, her face decorated with stars and swirls fashioned from glitter, and a pair of pink, sparkly deeley boppers bobbing around on top of her head.

"Look at me! I'm a fairy princess!" Molly held out her skirt and curtseyed.

"And a gorgeous one, too!" said Jess.

"Don't tell me Betty's in there?" Charlotte's eyes read the board outside the tent.

"Yep. Fingers crossed, she'll be out in a minute feeling like a new woman."

"Well, let's hope so," said Charlotte. "Poor Bet—fancy fretting over something for sixty years. I still can't believe that she…"

The tent flap flew open and Betty stumbled out, her face ashen, her usually bright eyes dull.

"So, did everything go… Bet, are you alright?" Ava held out a hand to steady her.

"Oh, my goodness, oh my!" Betty flopped down onto a nearby bench, her fingers clenched tightly around the strap of her handbag.

"Betty, what's wrong?"

"That man. That m‑man. He…he told me that…"

"What? What did he tell you?" Harriett urged.

"He told me that a connection to a secret admirer will put my life in danger." She wrung her hands. "It's exactly the same prediction as last time! He didn't even have a crystal ball, he read my cards. How could that happen if there wasn't at least *some* truth to it? And *don't* try to tell me it's nothing to worry about—not this time!"

Jess broke the silence. "Well, I don't know *how* it's happened but I'm sure it's just a fluke. I hope you're not going to let it spook you for the next goodness knows how many years, are you?"

Betty ferreted in her bag for her sunglasses. "That's all very well for you to say, love. I don't have as many years ahead of me as you and I'd prefer it if my remaining time on earth is devoid of anything that may be detrimental to my health."

"Oh, Betty, Jess is right. It's a coincidence, isn't it?" said Laura. "Fortune tellers have been giving out variations of the same predictions since I was a girl. The only thing that's changed is that they don't look nearly as intimidating as they used to. I mean, it just depends how you interpret what they tell you. You could most likely twist any prediction to be what you wanted to hear, if you wanted to hear it badly enough."

"Well, I can assure you," said Betty firmly, "I had no desire to hear that my life is in danger. And, before you say anything, it wasn't the way I interpreted it, that's exactly what he said—"in danger.""

"But what on earth could possibly happen to you?" Laura continued to reassure her. "We're all here with you and you're surrounded by people back home. And anyway, your secret admirer seems to have disappeared off the face of the earth, with no forwarding address, so I really think it's best if you just try to put all this out of your mind. Honestly, it's just a fluke, Bet."

Everyone murmured in agreement, offering words of encouragement.

There was no basis to the fortune teller's prediction.

Nothing to worry about.

Just a coincidence.

They walked on, idly browsing the stalls. Betty even forced a smile and waved as Molly flew past on the Merry Go Round.

The sun was hot on her skin but she couldn't help but shiver as the uneasy feeling she'd last felt sixty years before began to creep over her once again.

ooooooo

"Aah, this is the life. I don't know why we haven't done this before but we should definitely do it again," said Leo.

The sailing boat rocked with the gentle lull of the waves in the spot where Charlotte's godfather, Garrett Walton, had dropped anchor, away from the hustle and bustle closer to the shore.

"Wonder what the girls are doing?" Charlotte's husband, and St. Eves' Detective Chief Inspector, Nathan Costello, threw the crust from his sandwich into the sea, its surface as calm as a pond, and watched as it bobbed and jumped before finally being dragged under by the fish that descended upon it within seconds.

"Well, if I know Ava," said Harry, cursing under his breath as he reeled in yet another empty line, "she'll be organising the entire trip. I wouldn't be surprised if she took a whistle and clipboard with her."

"And a megaphone," Leo chuckled. "And Harriett will be rebelling, and Betty will be mediating and going along with whatever everyone else wants to do." He took a slice of pork pie from its foil package and demolished it in one bite. "You know how easy-going she is."

Nathan propped himself up on an elbow. "Well, Molly and Charlotte are having the time of their lives. I spoke to Molly last night and she said she wants to stay there forever." Stretched out on a towel on the deck, Nathan held a cold bottle of beer to his cheek. "Charlotte even suggested that we all go down for a few days before the end of the summer."

"Yeah, Laura said they were all enjoying themselves." Garrett spoke fondly of his wife. "Betty's been pretty fed up, though—they didn't manage to track down that guy they went looking for, did you know?"

"Yes, Harriett mentioned it when she called," said Leo. "Shame they went all that way for nothing, particularly as the whole point of the trip was so that Betty would feel better about some ancient prophecy from decades ago." He rolled his eyes.

Garrett swigged from a water bottle and threw the remains of his lunch into the sea to be devoured in seconds by a school of rapacious fish.

"It's no wonder I haven't had a bite all afternoon with you two around," grumbled Harry.

"Sorry, mate. Guess it's just not your day today," said Garrett. "In any case, we should be thinking about getting back."

Nathan's lips stretched in a cavernous yawn. "Yeah, I suppose so. Pity, I could stay out here all day. You okay?"

"Hmmm, feels like the anchor's got something caught on it. It's sluggish coming up." Garrett pulled the rope vertically up through the water. "Feels like something big. I can feel... Oh my God! Nathan, look!"

Caught on the anchor, and becoming clearer with every inch of its journey to the ocean's surface, were the remains of a human skeleton.

ooooooo

"Well, that's put a dampener on the afternoon, I don't mind telling you."

A fisherman for decades, nothing to come out of the sea had ever troubled Garrett in the slightest, but his latest haul had unsettled him no end.

"I was never very good at biology," said Nathan, "but I think it's a man. And by the look of him, he's been through the wars—he's pretty mangled."

The battered skeleton lay on the deck. A large portion of the skull was missing, along with most of the jaws, the feet and numerous other bones which were either broken, or had become otherwise detached during its time in the sea.

"Wonder who it is?" said Harry.

"Well, by the look of him, he's been in the water for some time," said Leo. "And that's a big old dent in his head. And look at all those broken bones. Wonder if he fell from one of the cliffs along the shoreline? Or jumped, maybe?"

"He could just have been buffeted about by the sea," said Harry. "Who knows how many times he could have been washed up against the rocks? I reckon some of those big ones in the coves just off the shore could do some pretty serious damage."

Garrett nodded. "You're right—they could. I've lost count of the number of boats that have run aground and sunk there over the years. Anyway, what happens now?"

Nathan crouched over the bones. "We'll see if we can ID him from the missing person's database although I doubt it'll be easy from what's left. And then we'll trace his family, if we can. I'd like to think someone's been missing him." He leaned forward and inspected the skeleton at closer quarters. "I don't like the look of those head injuries one bit. I'd like to know if they were inflicted before, or after he died. If he got them *before* he went into the water, I want to know how."

"Looks like most of his teeth have been broken," said Harry. "That'll hinder your chances of getting an ID from dental records, won't it?"

Nathan bent down for a closer look at the skull. "Hmm, a lot have been broken but if we can get an idea of who it is from missing persons, and get hold of some x-rays, a forensic dentist will be able to match them against what's left of the teeth. It'd probably be easier if they were complete but it'll still be enough to get an ID from."

"You aware of anyone who's missing from around here?" asked Garrett.

"No one springs to mind although there's every chance he isn't from St. Eves, or even this county. Or even this *country*, come to that. You know the sea better than I do, Garrett. The current could have carried him for miles. And goodness knows how long he's been in the sea. We'll just have to wait and see what we can come up with. If we can't find trace any dental records, we'll have to hope we can get an ID some other way."

"What a place to end up." A shiver ran though Garrett and he reached for his sweatshirt. "Can we cover him up with something? Doesn't seem right to have him on display like that." Pulling a tarpaulin from the under-seat compartment, he placed it over the skeleton.

He raked his fingernails across his stubbled jaw. "No disrespect, but do you think we can get him off here pretty quick? It's bad luck to have a dead body on board, see." He held up a hand. "And, yes, before you say anything, I know it's a skeleton but, in my book, that's the same thing." He shuddered again and crossed himself. "And God rest his soul, whoever he is."

CHAPTER FIVE

"Am I glad to see you."

Charlotte settled comfortably into Nathan's arms as Pippin and Panda each selected a couch on which to sprawl after the long drive home and Molly emptied the contents of her rucksack onto the rug.

"Daddy, daddy, look! This is a drawing I did of Ava when she fell asleep in the deckchair. Can you see? She's got her mouth open." She giggled behind her fingers.

"It's very good." Nathan nodded his approval. "What's that thing on her nose?"

"Huh? Oh that. It's a bee."

"A bee? Was it really on her nose, or did you just add it to your picture?"

"No, it was really there. It was a really *big* one, too."

"And you didn't wake her up to tell her?"

Molly raised an eyebrow and met Nathan's enquiring gaze. "Er, bees sting, you know, Daddy. I didn't want to get too close. It was okay though—Ava's snoring scared it away."

Nathan chuckled. "It's good to have you both home."

Charlotte yawned and stretched her back. "Right, Molly. Half an hour more with Daddy and then dinner, bath time and bed." She yawned again as the drive home took its toll. "I know you haven't seen her for a while, Nathan, but I don't want her to get over‑tired because then she won't sleep at all."

"No worries." Nathan picked Molly up and gave her a cuddle. "How about *I* put you to bed tonight, Mol? Then we can spend a little more time together and you can tell me all about your trip."

"Yaay!" Molly blew a raspberry on his cheek. "I'll just get my collection of stones and shells out of my bag so I can show them to you."

"How were things while we were away?" Charlotte kicked off her shoes and started to sort through the dirty laundry. "Anything exciting happen?"

"Oh, you know, this and that." He pointed to Molly and mouthed, "I'll tell you later."

ooooooo

"A skeleton? Oh, that's horrible! Do you have any idea who it is?"

With Molly tucked up in bed and sound asleep, Charlotte and Nathan sat down to a late dinner.

"Not yet but we're checking missing persons and I've asked Wendy Myers if she can take a look. Most of the skull and the jaws have gone, and there are a lot of broken or missing bones, so I don't know what she'll be able to tell me but I'd like her opinion on the head injuries.

"The fact that it's a skeleton is going to make an ID that much harder but Wendy's the best forensic pathologist I know so I'm hoping she'll be able to give us something to go on. Even if she can tell us how old he was, it'll help narrow down the search on missing persons. Anyway, let's not talk about work." Nathan tipped his glass to Charlotte's. "How was Betty by the end of your trip? Was she very fed up about not finding her friend?"

"Yeah, she was really down about it for a while and that's not like her at all. He obviously meant a lot to her because she said she would have loved to have got together with him. It's a real shame he never told her how he felt about her when he came to live at Sunny Days. Such a waste when they could have had a few years together, at least."

"Yeah. It's a pity. Still, if someone ups and disappears the way he did, without so much as a goodbye, perhaps she was better off without him."

Charlotte yawned as she poured another glass of wine. "Actually, between you and me, I'm quite glad we *didn't* find him. It was bad enough when she got the first prediction that a connection to an admirer was going to put her life in danger, but getting the same one again has really shaken her up. And Patrick's not even around. Can you imagine how much more jittery she'd be if he was? She'd be forever looking over her shoulder."

"Well, maybe the admirer isn't Patrick? Maybe it's someone else?"

"No, Betty said he's the only one. And, according to what she said was in those letters, it's pretty obvious that he was in love with her."

"That's a sad story about his sister," said Nathan. "You can understand why the family moved away after that." His phone vibrated across the table and he peered at the display. "Speak of the devil—it's Wendy. Sorry, love, I'd better take this. Hi, I was just talking about you. No, it's okay, go on. Oh, that's great—that should help a lot as far as missing persons go. And it'll give us something to go on until you can tell us some more, and we can hopefully get hold of some dental records. Thanks for letting me know. Yep, speak to you soon." He ended the call and reached for his wine glass.

"Must have been important to call at this time of night," said Charlotte, with another yawn. "What's up?"

"Apparently, one of our John Doe's legs is a bit shorter than the other so he must have had a limp. Now we know that, we might have more luck finding out who he is if we narrow our search on the missing person's database to just sift out the people who've got a limp."

"Oh, right." Charlotte's eyelids, which had been becoming increasingly heavier throughout dinner, shot open as she sat bolt upright in her chair.

"Did I dream what you just said?"

"Hmm?" said Nathan, sipping his wine.

"What did you just say?"

"What? About our John Doe?"

"*Yes*, about your John Doe. What did you say about his legs?"

"Oh. Wendy said one of his legs is shorter than the other, so he must have had a limp. Why's that interesting?"

Charlotte jumped up from her chair. "Because I know who it is. Oh no! Poor Betty!"

"What are you talking about? And what's Betty got to do with it?"

"It's Patrick Jones. Betty's Patrick, the guy we went looking for." Charlotte paced up and down, her hands in her hair. "One of his legs was shorter than the other. Some hereditary condition, apparently." She slumped back down in the chair. "No wonder we couldn't find him. It all makes sense, doesn't it? Him disappearing without a trace and not saying goodbye, not leaving a forwarding address, not answering his phone and not being at Sutton's Folly. Betty's going to be devastated. You should have seen her face when she found out that he wasn't in either of those retirement homes."

"Are you sure about this?" Nathan reached for his phone again.

"Of course I am! I've heard so much about Patrick Jones over the past week, I feel like I know him myself."

"Well, this puts a totally different light on things." Nathan scrolled through his contact list. "We thought we had a John Doe and nothing to go on but, suddenly, it looks like we *could* have an ID and a whole list of questions that need to be answered. I'd better make a couple of calls. Sorry, darling." He left his unfinished dinner on the table and disappeared into the living room.

So much for not talking about work. Her appetite having deserted her, Charlotte pushed her plate away, her thoughts turning to Betty. If her reaction to not finding Patrick in Sutton's Folly was anything to go by, she was going to be inconsolable when she found out about this latest development.

"Right, Fiona and I are going to visit Cooper Anderson at Sunny Days tomorrow," said Nathan as he reappeared. "Seeing as that was the last place we know of that Patrick Jones lived, it's a good a place as any to start finding out what might have happened to him. And now that Wendy's on the case, we should know more in a few days."

oooooo

Charlotte kicked off the duvet and flicked a switch at the side of the bed to turn the ceiling fan up to full speed.

"Can't sleep?" murmured Nathan from beside her.

"No. I'm too hot and I can't stop thinking about that poor man's skeleton being pulled out of the sea. It's just too awful to even think about how he ended up like that." She turned her pillow over and punched it before laying her cheek against the cool cotton. "And I can't stop thinking about how Betty's going to take the news, either."

She tossed and turned for another minute before sitting up in bed, all prospects of sleep gone. "Do you think we could pop round to her place and tell her about it before the papers have it plastered all over the front pages and it's on every news channel? I think we should, Nathan. We know we can trust her and she won't tell anyone we've spoken to her if we ask her not to. You'd have to go a long way before you found anyone as trustworthy as Betty. What do you think?"

Nathan opened an eye. "Charlotte, why do you keep saying, "we"? There is no "we" in a police investigation. It's happening again, isn't it? You're already involved and we don't even know what we're dealing with."

Over the years, he'd become used to Charlotte's enthusiastic interest in his work—in fact, her input had been helpful on more than one occasion—but she'd become involved a little too deeply at times and he felt much happier when he knew she was out of harm's way.

The force of his toothpaste-scented sigh as it hit Charlotte in the face conveyed his exasperation.

"Oh, don't be like that." She prodded his shoulder. "You know I'm right. And, if you want to know anything about Patrick Jones, what better person to ask than Betty? Talk about a reliable source. You'll know that everything she tells you is accurate. Er, hello." She jabbed at him again. "Are you still awake?"

"Unfortunately, yes. I am. Okay, remind me in the morning." Nathan pulled her to him and planted a kiss on her lips. "Goodnight."

Charlotte turned her pillow over again and settled down. "Actually," she said after five minutes, "it might be better if we—I mean, you—talk to her here. I'll pop round tomorrow morning and invite her to dinner tomorrow night. That's a better idea than us—I mean, you—going round to her place, don't you think? Nathan?"

"Hmmm. Whatever you say..."
Within a minute, he was snoring loudly.

CHAPTER SIX

"Good morning, Mr. Anderson. I'm DCI Costello and this is DS Farrell. We'd like to speak to you in connection with an investigation. Can we come in, please?"

At the Sunny Days retirement complex, Cooper Anderson stood aside and waved Nathan and Fiona into the reception hall. "I assume this is about that skeleton you found?"

Nathan's brow shot up. "Why would you think we were here about that?"

"Because in all the years we've managed the complex, we've never had a visit from the police. Then, a skeleton turns up and, suddenly, you're on the doorstep. It's too much of a coincidence." Cooper smiled. "Wouldn't you say?"

"Well, that's one way of looking at it, I suppose," said Nathan. "How did you find out about it, out of interest?"

"Word gets around quickly, you know...especially if my wife's got anything to do with it. She was walking along the seafront when it was brought ashore. She saw the crowd on the beach and went down to see what was going on. Within ten minutes, it was all around the complex. Mind you, you know what it's like in a town like this—you can't keep news like that quiet for long."

"No, I suppose not." Nathan assessed Cooper through guarded eyes. "Although we're not actually here to talk about that. We'd like to ask some questions about an ex-resident of yours. We won't keep you long, I'm sure. Just a few questions."

"Oh, I see. Well, please make yourselves comfortable." Cooper ushered them into an office filled with dark wood furniture, the smell of wax polish, and French windows which opened onto lush gardens. "Shall I organise some tea?"

"No, thank you. We'll try to take as little of your time as possible." Fiona settled herself in one of the armchairs and took out her notebook.

"So, who's this resident you want to know about?"

"Patrick Jones. We're particularly interested in finding out more about the circumstances of his departure."

"Patrick Jones? My goodness, he's awfully popular all of a sudden. You're the second person to ask about him in the last couple of weeks."

"Oh? Who else has asked?"

Cooper stroked his chin. "I can't remember her name but she was looking for him on behalf of a friend. Older woman, very well-turned-out, called me "dear" which was rather nice—reminded me of my grandmother. No-one's called me that in years. Can't recall her name, though."

A smile played on Nathan's lips. "That's okay, I think I can guess who it is from your description."

"Why do you want to know about him, anyway?" asked Cooper. "He hasn't lived here for years."

"We're just interested to find out what you remember about him leaving Sunny Days, if you could help with that," said Fiona.

Cooper settled himself on the edge of the desk. "There's not much to remember, really. He just disappeared in the middle of the night, without any warning. I wasn't very happy about it because, if a resident moves on, they're supposed to give one month's notice. And, unless the circumstances are unavoidable, they're supposed to clear the bungalows of all the furniture and leave them clean and tidy for the next resident. They're unfurnished when they take them on, you see.

"Anyway, he just cleared off one night without a word; no goodbye, no forwarding address, no nothing, *and* he left all his stuff here. We had to pay to have the place cleared out and cleaned from top to bottom. It cost me a pretty penny, I can tell you, and I wasn't pleased. In fact, I was furious about it."

"Yes, I can imagine. And when was the last time you saw him, do you remember?"

"Now *that*," Cooper wagged a finger, "I *can* tell you. It was in the club house the day before he left. I only remember it so clearly because when we realised he'd gone, I recalled that being the last time I'd seen him."

"Did you ever try to locate him after he left?"

"I called him a couple of times but he never answered. I won't repeat the message I left on his answerphone. Believe me, if I'd known where he'd gone, I would have sent him an invoice for what he owed me—I might even have gone to get the money from him myself."

"Were you surprised when he left?"

"Yes, of course I was, but everyone knew he wasn't much for goodbyes so, although it was unexpected, it made sense that he'd just slipped away without a fuss."

"And you've no idea where he would have gone?"

Cooper blew out his cheeks. "None. He used to say that he wanted to live out his days in the countryside. He liked the solitude, he said. He never said where, though."

"I see." Fiona scribbled in her notebook. "Would you happen to know his next of kin? Or did you have any emergency contact details for him?"

"Erm, he did give us someone's details when he first arrived... Now, let me think." Cooper tapped the pads of his fingers together. "I'm pretty sure it was a cousin, but he didn't live in the UK. Canada rings a bell. Yes, I'm sure Patrick said he lived in Canada. And that he'd been over there to visit him before he came to Sunny Days."

"We'd be interested to see those details if you still have a file on Mr. Jones."

"Well, I'm sure we still have a file," said Cooper, "but they had a disagreement and Patrick asked us to remove his cousin's name from his records. He said he no longer considered him as his next of kin. I've no idea what happened but it must have been something pretty serious—he said he hoped he never saw him again."

Fiona looked up from her notebook and met Cooper's eye. "Mr. Anderson, we have reason to believe that someone, or something, may have stopped Mr. Jones from leaving St. Eves. Would you know anything about that?"

Cooper's brows dipped. "Look, I don't know what you're inferring but he didn't leave his wallet or passport behind, and all his clothes were gone, so I assume he packed a bag with the intention of leaving. It certainly didn't seem to me as though anyone had snaffled him away in the middle of the night, if that's what you mean." His face paled. "Good God! You're not here because you think that skeleton is anything to do with Patrick, are you?"

"If you could just answer the question, please, Mr. Anderson?"

"Oh. yes, of course. No, I have no idea who, or what, could have stopped him from leaving. I assumed he'd just upped and left the way he did because he wanted to move on, but couldn't be bothered with the hassle of clearing out the bungalow.

"What happened to the belongings he left behind?" asked Nathan.

"We got rid of most of them. We had to pay a man with a van to come and clear the place. And we sold the rest. You know, to help recoup what we'd had to pay for the clearance." Cooper ran a hand from his top lip down to his neck. "Look, Detective Chief Inspector, I can assure you that, while the circumstances of Patrick's disappearance may seem strange to you, there was absolutely no reason for us to believe that anything untoward had happened. If we had, I would have informed the police immediately. This retirement complex is our livelihood and some of the residents are very wealthy—as was Patrick—and we can't afford to have any bad publicity." He shifted awkwardly on the desk. "I know I had a lot of bad things to say about him after he left, and you'll probably hear about them from some of the residents.

I'm not very good at keeping my feelings to myself sometimes, I'm afraid." He grimaced. "But, whatever happened to him, it was nothing to do with me."

"Well, thank you for the admission, Mr. Anderson, although we're not actually accusing you of anything—just asking some questions."

"Yes, of c·course," Cooper stammered, "I know that. I just wanted to make it clear."

"I understand." Fiona smiled. "Just one more thing for now. Would it be possible for us to see Patrick's file? You said you thought you still have it."

Cooper raked his hair from his forehead. "Yes, I'm sure we do but I'll have to call Ellen, my wife. She deals with that area of the business. I'll call her now, shall I?"

"If you would, that'd be helpful. Thank you." Fiona drummed her fingers on the arm of the chair and watched Nathan watch Cooper.

"Hi, it's me. Could you come to the office right away, please? No, can you come now? It's urgent. And can you bring Patrick Jones's file with you. Patrick Jones. Yes. Look, you'll find out when you get here. Okay, thanks." Cooper put down the phone and sidled back around the desk. "She won't be too long—she's helping out on housekeeping today."

An awkward silence descended upon the room, broken by the rustle of a pile of papers as they

Sherri Bryan

fluttered from the desk to the floor in the wake of
Ellen's melodramatic entrance.

"Where's the fire, Coop? What's so urgent? And
why do you need this?"

She held up the file, stopping short when she
saw that she and Cooper had company. "Oh. I know
you, you're the DCI, aren't you? I saw you on the beach
the other day." She smiled and stepped forward, her
arm outstretched. "Your wife has the café on the
marina, doesn't she? Very nice to meet you, I'm Ellen
Anderson." She extended her arm to Fiona. "And you
are?"

"DS Farrell. Good to meet you."

Ellen's gaze went from Nathan to Fiona to
Cooper. "Is there a problem?"

Cooper cleared his throat. "Actually, it's about
the skeleton that was found. They think it might be
Patrick Jones."

Ellen's hands flew to her cheeks. "Oh, my
goodness, no! That's awful. Whatever happened to
him?"

"We didn't actually say that, Mr. Anderson."
Nathan shot Cooper a glare. "It's still very early in our
investigation and we haven't officially confirmed who
it is. We're just trying to establish what happened to
Mr. Jones after he left here."

Ellen dropped onto the end of the couch. "Yes, of course, I understand. How can I help?"

"Do you remember the last time you saw Mr. Jones?"

"Oh, er, I don't, I'm afraid. It was probably in the club house but it could just as well have been out in the grounds or in town. I really don't remember. I'm sorry."

"Not to worry. If you happen to recall anything, perhaps you could let us know." Fiona made a note. "Now, we appreciate that under normal circumstances, you'd want to maintain a degree of confidentiality regarding your residents but, as Patrick Jones left here four years ago, I wonder if you'd be willing to share some of his information with us? Would you know the dentist he used, for example?"

"Um, I don't recall off the top of my head if it was our in-house dentist, or one from the town. Let me just have a look." She flipped through the buff-coloured folder. "We'd archived the file but it's all still here," she explained. "Considering Patrick's age he was in remarkably good health. He was one of the few residents we never had to call a doctor for. You know apart from his leg which, to be honest, was barely even a handicap to him, he wasn't troubled by any ailments, as far as I know. Was he, Coop?"

"Not to my knowledge. He was certainly a strong old boy and he got around perfectly well with his walking stick. Any luck, Ellen?"

She shook her head. "Sorry. He never used our in-house dentist. Or any of our in-house medical facilities, come to that. Quite a few of the residents suffer from the usual aches and pains, at the very least, but I don't think I recall Patrick ever having as much as a headache. That should tell you what good shape he was in."

"I see. You said you'd left a message on his mobile phone after he left, Mr. Anderson. Would you have a record of the number on file?"

"Er, let me see. Yes, here we are. It's 07911 654321."

The door burst opened and a young man wearing tennis shorts and a t-shirt emblazoned with a picture of Elvis Presley rushed in, sugar from the doughnut he was eating stuck to his cheeks.

"Dad, can you lend me £20 until tomorrow? I'm going to St. Matlock with Wayne and Del and I need some cash." Suddenly aware that they had company, he blushed when he saw Nathan and Fiona.

"Oh, sorry, I didn't know anyone was here." He ran a hand through his spiky black hair and dropped his gaze to the floor.

"Don't worry, son, you're not interrupting anything important." Cooper took out his wallet and handed over a fifty pound note.

"But I only want..."

Cooper flapped the protest away. "Just take it. Pay me back when you can. You're only young once and £20 doesn't get you anything these days." He patted his son on the back before introducing him. "DCI Costello, DS Farrell, this is our son, Paul."

Paul's face turned from scarlet to grey in an instant. "You're the police?"

"We are indeed. Nice to meet you," said Fiona.

"How do you do." Nathan held out his hand.

"Nice to meet you," Paul mumbled, barely raising his eyes. He turned to Cooper. "Why are they here?"

"Just asking about someone who was a resident a few years ago. You probably won't remember him— Patrick Jones."

Paul frowned. "Patrick Jones? Er, no, no, I don't recognise the name. Why are they asking about him, anyway?"

"Just part of an investigation, son. Nothing for you to be concerned about."

Paul shoved the £50 note into his pocket. "I should be getting off. The guys are waiting for me in town."

"You'll be home for dinner, won't you?" said Ellen. "Jem and Gavin are coming over."

"Yeah, okay. I'll be back by nine."

"By eight, please. And your aunt Holly's coming over too."

Paul raised his head for the first time. "Aunt Holly's coming? Why? Why's *she* coming?"

"Because *you're* home, I expect. She hasn't seen you since you got back. Why don't you invite Wayne and Del?"

Paul chewed on his lip. "No, it's okay. They'll have their own stuff to do. Anyway, I'd better go."

"Eight o' clock! And don't eat any more doughnuts or you won't want your dinner." Ellen called after Paul as he disappeared from the room. "He's been addicted to the things for years," she explained. "And I know I probably fuss over him a little more than I should but he's back from college for a few weeks and I can't help it; he's my baby and I haven't got used to him being away yet. Not sure I ever will. He was our little surprise, you know—totally unplanned." She beamed and it was Cooper's turn to look embarrassed.

"Ellen, I'm sure the detectives aren't interested in our procreation history." He scratched the back of his neck and stared out of the French windows.

Ignoring him completely, Ellen continued. "Two things about Paul; he's always adored his sister—our daughter, Jemima—he's sooo protective of her, you know, and he's always been incredibly shy. He's getting better, though. At one time, he was scared of his own shadow but since he's been at college, he's coming out of his shell at last. Mind you, Jemima's not the most outgoing of people, is she, Coop? She's not nearly as bad as Paul, though."

"Jemima's fine when she's on her own," snapped Cooper. "It's that Gavin who holds her back. Her confidence has taken a nosedive since she married him."

Ellen shook her head. "If I had £1 for every time Coop grumbles about Gavin, I wouldn't be running a retirement complex in St. Eves, I can assure you. I'd be sunning myself on a tropical beach, waiting for a waiter in a sarong to bring me a cocktail in half a coconut shell. The poor man can't do a thing right in his eyes." She tucked a strand of hair that had come loose from her crocodile clip behind her ear. "Anyway, where were we?"

"You were telling us that Patrick Jones never used your in-house medical facilities."

"Ah, yes, that's right. I'm sorry I can't be of more help," said Ellen, looking at her watch. "Look, I'm sorry to run but we're terribly busy. If you've finished with me, I really need to get back to work—I've left Jemima on her own. Speaking of which, she's going to be devastated when she hears about this. She was terribly fond of Patrick."

"Was she?"

"Yes, she and he were very friendly. Much to Gavin's annoyance, I should say. Patrick was never his favourite person, you see, and he didn't take at all kindly to their friendship. Silly, really. I mean, Patrick was over forty years older than Jem. I don't know why on earth Gavin used to get so uptight about it but he still gives her a hard time whenever Patrick's name is mentioned."

"Is it likely that she would have seen him before he left?"

"I've no idea," said Ellen, "but she saw him most days so I expect so. Whether she'll be able to remember anything going back that far, though, I really couldn't tell you."

"I can call her now, if you'd like to have a chat with her," offered Cooper. "You can speak to her here. Would you like me to call her?"

"Don't worry, I'll let her know." Ellen stood to leave.

"Before you go, would you mind if we borrowed that file?" asked Fiona. "There could be something in there that could help us."

Ellen exchanged a glance with Cooper and shrugged. "Well, I don't see why not—it's not as though there's any sensitive information in it. We don't need it any more and it's in a good cause, I suppose."

She handed over the file, laughed a tinkly laugh and went on her way.

ooooooo

"Mum said that the skeleton you found the other day is Patrick Jones! Is that true?"

Jemima Campbell's eyes were twice their usual size in her pale face as she burst into the office.

Fiona sighed. "Mrs. Campbell, we specifically said that we haven't yet officially identified it. For now, we're simply interested in trying to get a clearer picture of what happened to Mr. Jones after he left Sunny Days. Now, I know it's been a while, but do you recall the last time you saw him?"

Jemima gave a distracted nod and kicked off her shoes before lowering herself, cross-legged, into an armchair.

"Course I do. I remember it like it was yesterday. That's what happens when friends hurt you, you know, you never really get over it. It was in town; late afternoon the day before he left. I thought at the time that he was acting a little odd—sort of secretive—which wasn't like him at all. I could see that he had an envelope tucked inside his jacket but I've no idea what it was. I waited for him to tell me but he didn't, so I didn't ask him. I assumed he either didn't want me to see it, or he didn't want to talk about it, so I didn't push it. It was the only time he'd ever acted like he wasn't pleased to see me. Anyway, we walked back to Sunny Days together and then we went our separate ways. The last thing he said to me was that I should take care of myself and get away from Gavin before he ruined my life. He didn't think Gavin was good enough for me, you see."

"Hmpf, that's one thing Patrick Jones and I agreed on, at least," mumbled Cooper as he doodled on the desk blotter.

"And did your husband ever voice an opinion on Mr. Jones?"

Jemima arched her brows in an exaggerated manner. "Er, you could say that. And it wasn't very complimentary. He was jealous because I thought so much of him. He thought my relationship with Patrick was weird." Her eyes widened again and she shook her head wildly. "Not that we had a relationship in *that* sense of the word, you understand. What I mean is that Gavin didn't like that Patrick and I were friends. He couldn't understand how a woman of my age and a man of Patrick's age could have anything in common. But we did. He was an amazing man—I used to tell him anything and everything. If I wanted advice, he'd give it, but if I just wanted to get stuff off my chest, he'd listen without judging. And he couldn't *stand* Gavin—he used to tell me to leave him almost every day. You know, sometimes I was so fed up, I used to tell him that, if I had the money, I would.

"He was such a good friend—I still don't understand why he left without saying goodbye. Even after all these years, I still miss him." She leaned her head back and took a deep breath. "You know, it's nice to be able to talk about him to someone without them thinking I'm a weirdo. We really were fond of each other. He was like a granddad to me—such a sweetie. I still get upset when I think about him." A lone tear spilled onto her cheek and Cooper handed her a box of tissues.

Fiona snapped her notebook shut. "Thank you for your time, Mrs. Campbell. That's all for now but if there's anything else you can help us with, we'll be in touch."

ooooooo

"That young lad doesn't seem very keen on his aunt Holly, does he?" said Fiona. "Did you notice his reaction when his mum told him she was going round for dinner tonight?"

"And did you see his face when he saw us?" said Nathan. "I thought he was going to pass out, the way all the colour drained away. He could only just bring himself to shake my hand. Talk about not feeling wanted—if I had an inferiority complex, I might have been upset."

Fiona laughed. "What now, Chief?"

"Well, Ben was going to try to speak to Dr. Talbot this morning to see if he can tell us anything which may help to further corroborate that the skeleton actually is Patrick Jones. Until we have more info from forensics, and we can get our hands on some dental records, anything the doc can tell us will help. We'll wait to see what Ben comes back with before we do anything else."

ooooooo

"Morning, Ben. Long time, no see. How's things? And how's Jess? She okay?"

Dr. Talbot jangled a large bunch of keys as he attempted to chain his bike to the rack outside the surgery. "I really must sort through these one day. I've no idea what most of them are for. Takes me forever to find the only three keys I actually use. Ah, that's it. You're a bit early for an appointment, by the way. You know we don't open for another hour? Or are you waiting to speak to me?"

"Yes, I am, actually," said Ben. "Could you spare me five minutes?"

"As long as it's only five—I've got a hellishly busy morning. Just going to change, won't be a sec." He went into the small bathroom off his consulting room. "What is it you want to know?" he called through the door.

"I wanted to ask you about someone who used to live in St. Eves. Patrick Jones. Did you know him?"

"Hmmm, Patrick Jones. Flo and Henry's son, you mean? What about him?"

"Was he a patient of yours?"

"Well, he was registered at the surgery but I never once saw him as a patient. He used to come to appointments with his parents but I never saw him on his own. I got to know his mother quite well, though. I was very sorry when she passed away."

Dr. Talbot reappeared in a suit, complete with waistcoat and tie, his preferred attire regardless of the season. "Like his father, one of his legs was shorter than the other—a hereditary condition commonly known as Structural Short Leg Syndrome which caused him to walk with a limp.

"He also suffered with occasional pain from osteophytes on one of his shoulders. Sorry, bone spurs is the common name," he said, in response to Ben's blank look. "They're growths on the bones. He asked me about them at his mother's funeral whilst a number of other people were present, so I feel I can mention it to you with a clear conscience that I'm not in violation of doctor/patient privilege. He wanted to know if there was anything he could do about them. I told him about the treatment and surgery options and that was the end of the conversation."

He looked at his watch, a twinkle in his mischievous eyes. "And that, I believe, is your five minutes up. Tell Jess I send my regards, won't you?"

ooooooo

"So, we know that Patrick left Sunny Days four years ago without a word," said Fiona, quickly filling Ben in on developments. "It seems likely that he *intended* to leave because he packed up the things he wanted to take. And we know that, despite attempts to call him, his phone wasn't answered. We also know that he has a cousin in Canada who he had some kind of dispute with which led to them breaking ties."

"And we know that he suffered from a hereditary condition that caused one of his legs to be shorter than the other and that he also suffered with bone spurs on his shoulder," said Ben. "The fact that Dr. Talbot never saw him as a patient leads me to believe that he must have been in pretty good health."

"Well, that would certainly back up what Ellen and Cooper Anderson told us," said Fiona.

"We also know that the Anderson's daughter, Jemima, was very friendly with him. Just a mutual friendship—nothing to indicate it was anything more than that. And we know from Betty that he was very popular with other residents although, not so much with Cooper Anderson. And Cooper's son-in-law, Gavin, wasn't a fan either, because of Patrick's friendship with his wife," said Nathan. "Right, we need to speak to Gavin asap. Perhaps you two could do that while I go back to the station and take a look through this." He patted Patrick Jones' Sunny Days file. "I'll catch up with you later."

oooooo

Having returned to Sunny Days to be told that Gavin Campbell was at a meeting with local supplier, Mobility Methods, Ben and Fiona pulled up outside the purpose-built office bearing the company's name.

"Well, that must be his van," said Ben. "I can't see any others with multiple Sunny Days Retirement Complex stickers on the back windscreen. We'll wait ten minutes before going in to let him know we're here, shall we?"

"Sounds good to me." Fiona squinted through the tinted-glass frontage. "Is that him at the reception desk through there, can you see?"

"Well it's someone, but I've no idea if it's him," said Ben. "I've never seen him before. Have you?"

"A few times," said Fiona. "At the leisure centre when I've been for my Zumba class. Not that he's in it too," she stressed, "he goes to weight training on the same evening." She checked her watch. "Actually, let's go and wait inside. If that *is* him, maybe it'll hurry him along a bit."

The heavy glass door opened into a modern lobby, at one end of which stood a black marble reception desk attended by two flawlessly coiffured women with make-up to match.

Lounging against the desk was Gavin Campbell. His broad back and shoulders filled every inch of his shirt, his cropped hair hugged his head close.

"You can call that number any time, Letitia, and I'll be the only one who answers, so you'll never need to worry about my wife picking up—you get my meaning?"

He passed a slip of paper across the desk to a brunette with painted on eyebrows. She accepted it with the good grace reserved only for the most important of clients although her smile barely upturned the corners of her mouth.

"If you'll excuse me, Mr. Campbell." Letitia's relief was evident. "Can I help you?"

"Actually, it's Mr. Campbell we're here to see." Ben flashed his warrant card. "When you've finished whatever business you're conducting, of course."

"Oh, I think we're finished," said Letitia, discreetly scrunching up the piece of paper and tossing it into the waste bin.

Gavin looked Fiona and Ben up and down before pushing past. "Outside," he uttered, before stepping into the car park.

"We won't take much of your time, Mr. Campbell."

Gavin gave a low chuckle. "My mother-in-law called earlier to tell me the good news. Said Patrick Jones might have kicked the bucket and that you'd probably want to speak to me"

Ben raised an eyebrow. "Did she? I see."

"Yeah. She said the police had been snooping around asking questions. So, what do you want to know."

"Can you tell us when you last saw Patrick Jones?"

Gavin glared at Ben, his lips pursed in a narrow furrow. "Oh, come on! He left Sunny Days years ago— I've no idea when I last saw him. Do *you* remember what *you* were doing that long ago? I didn't make a habit of hanging out with him, you know. I thought he was an idiot. And a weirdo."

"And why was that?"

Gavin's lip curled. "Because of the way he used to hang around my wife, that's why. He was more than forty years older than her. I dread to think what the two of them used to get up to." He shuddered. "But I warned him off, don't worry about that. I told him that if he ever went near her again, I'd make sure she was the last woman he ever spoke to."

"You threatened him?" Ben frowned.

"Course I threatened him—he was messing about with my wife, wasn't he? But it was just words, wasn't it? I didn't actually *do* anything to the stupid old duffer. Not that I wouldn't have, mind you, given half a chance. I just never *got* the chance because he did a disappearing act, didn't he?" His face broke in a smug smile. "I reckon I must have frightened him off. Anyway, what're you asking *me* about him for?"

"We're speaking to everyone at Sunny Days, not just you."

"Well, you've spoken to me now so you can clear off. I can't tell you anything else 'cos I don't know anything else." He strolled to his van, turning before he opened the door. "Whatever happened to him, he got what he deserved, as far as I'm concerned. There are two things you should never mess with; another man's wife and another man's money." He winked and gave his nose a sharp tap. "Know what I mean?"

CHAPTER SEVEN

After dropping Molly at her dance class, Charlotte popped round to see Betty.

"Hello, Charlotte. Why, this is a lovely surprise. Nice to see a friendly face about the place for a change." Betty opened the door in the flowery overall she wore when she did the housework. "Come in, come in. I could do with an excuse to put the kettle on."

"Don't tell me everyone's still ignoring you?"

"I wish I could say they weren't, but yes, they are." Betty sighed as she put two mugs on a tray beside a sturdy china teapot. "It's ridiculous behaviour but what can I do? By the way, what d'you think about the skeleton the boys pulled out of the water on Sunday?"

"Oh, you've heard about it?"

"Yes, Leo and Harriett came round last night to tell me. Talk about a shock for poor Garrett. Leo said he went as white as a sheet."

"Er, yes, I know. It must have been terrible to see." Not wanting to get into a conversation about the grisly find until later, Charlotte changed the subject. "Um, I popped round to ask if you'd like to come for dinner this evening? And you can stay over, if you want to—you know, make a night of it. We never see you on your own and we keep saying it'd be nice to get together. How are you fixed?"

"You mean apart from sitting home and not talking to anyone?" Betty clapped her hands. "Charlotte, I'd love to come to dinner, thank you. But only if I can bring dessert."

"Honestly, there's no need," said Charlotte.

"Oh, okay. Just that I made a summer pudding yesterday with a pound of over-ripe berries there were selling off cheap at the market. It's been chilling all night in the fridge. It'd be a shame to have to eat it all on my own." Betty stole a sly peek at Charlotte.

Charlotte's eyes widened. Betty's legendary summer puddings were the stuff of dreams. "Oh, well, in that case..."

They laughed as Betty poured the tea.

ooooooo

"Come on, let's go and sit in the garden. It's still so warm out there." Charlotte put an arm around Betty's shoulder.

"Well, this is lovely, I must say. I wasn't really looking forward to spending the evening alone." Betty eased off her sandals and put her feet up on the edge of a raised flowerbed. "I was going to make do with an egg salad for dinner until you called round."

Molly came skidding out of the kitchen at top speed, Pippin and Panda at her heels, and flung her arms around Betty's waist.

"Betty! Have you come to play shops with us?" she asked, her lips a strange purple hue. "Erin and Esme are here—they're having a sleepover. I've just had a blueberry cookie from Molly's Muffins—would you like one?"

"What's Molly's Muffins?"

Molly rolled her eyes. "It's my play cake shop, of course."

Betty chuckled and smoothed the young girl's hair. "Perhaps a bit later, love. Let me rest my old bones in the sun for a while."

"'Kay." Undeterred, Molly ran back to her friends and her cake shop, barking dogs in tow, all three of them avoiding a collision with Nathan by inches as he brought out a jug of elderflower cordial. He shook his head and grinned.

"Honestly, it's like a madhouse in there sometimes. At least you can hear yourself think out here. And it's away from little ears."

Betty took the glass Nathan offered. "You got things you want to talk about-you'd rather Molly didn't hear?"

Nathan nodded. "There's no rush, though. We'll chat after dinner when the kids are upstairs."

ooooooo

With Molly, Esme and Erin safely ensconced upstairs, Nathan and Charlotte finally sat down with Betty.

"I'm really sorry. I wish there'd been an easy way to tell you. I know it's awful but we couldn't bear for you to have found out by reading about it in the paper, or seeing it on TV." Charlotte added another spoon of sugar to Betty's cup of strong tea.

"And it won't be long before it's all over the news because The Herald are on our heels for details." Nathan handed Betty his oversized cotton handkerchief. "As it is, one of their reporters was on the beach when we brought the remains ashore so they've been baying for information since then. It won't be long before they have it splattered across the front page.

"I just can't believe he's gone—not Patrick. He was such a character. You know that term, 'larger-than-life'? Well, that was Patrick, to an absolute tee." Betty dried her eyes.

"Are you up to answering a few questions?" asked Nathan. "Don't worry if you're not."

"Yes, that's okay. I don't mind." She gulped her tea and blew her nose.

"Do you remember much about the last time you saw him?"

"Oh yes. I saw him the evening before he left when I popped round to return a book he'd lent me. He was clearing out a few things and there was a painting on the couch that caught my eye and I said how much I liked it. He said he'd been planning on throwing it out but if I wanted it he'd much prefer me to have it. He even walked me back to my place and put it on the wall for me—told me to think of him whenever I looked at it and it would be as if he was right here with me. It's still above the fireplace now." She heaved a great sigh. "And that was the last time I saw him."

"Anything else you can think of?"

"Not really. it's such a shock, I just can't think straight." Betty wound the handkerchief around her finger. "All I can tell you is that, as far as we all knew, Patrick was very happy at Sunny Days and we were all delighted when he came to live there. I must admit, I was a little concerned when he first turned up— because of what that fortune teller told me, I mean— but, when he seemed more interested in Nora Tweedie than me, I eventually stopped worrying about it."

"And how did the other residents react to Patrick's arrival?"

"Oh, they loved him. He was popular, had no enemies and was the life and soul of the party. Everyone wanted to be his friend. He was just a genuinely lovely man and I can't think of anyone who would have wanted to harm him."

"Was there anything troubling him, do you know?" asked Nathan.

Betty fixed him with a watery-eyed glare. "Nathan Costello, if you're asking me if I think he did himself in, the answer's no. He just wouldn't have."

"Okay. Did he ever speak about his family?"

Betty nodded. "His parents were very religious, especially his dad. It's one of the reasons Patrick didn't wear a lift in his shoe—you know, one of those things that would have stopped him being lopsided? He told me his dad used to say, "If this is the way God made us, this is the way we're supposed to be and it's not for us to change it."

"They were very wealthy, too. Patrick was always treating us all to cream cakes and ice creams and when I asked him how he could afford it on a pension, he told me the inheritance from his parents had left him very well-off. His mother's side of the family had property and diamonds and goodness knows what. He didn't tell me in a boastful way, just very matter of factly. He was ever so generous—said there was no one he wanted to leave his money to, so he might as well spend it on making other people happy.

"Then there was his aunt, uncle and cousin in Canada. His aunt and uncle died years ago. Patrick never met them but after his own parents passed away, he went to visit his cousin for the first time. He was born in England but his family moved to Canada when he was a baby so he and Patrick had never met.

"Anyway, when he came back to the UK after his trip is when he turned up at Sunny Days. He said that seeing John, that was his cousin, had made him realise that he wanted to re-establish old ties, and be with people he knew.

"He never mentioned his sister at all. That poor girl—I expect Charlotte must have told you what happened to her?" Betty picked at her bowl of summer pudding. "I'm not sure I can do this justice. Maybe I'll have it later." She burst into tears again and Charlotte put her arm around her.

"Why did this have to happen? To Patrick, of all people? All he ever wanted was to enjoy life and help others—especially the ones who meant a lot to him. His friends were important, you see, because he'd lost almost all his family. That's why it was such a pity that he fell out with John, particularly as they'd got on so well in Canada."

"Ah, yes, I heard they'd had a disagreement," said Nathan. "What was it about, do you know?"

Betty blew her nose. "After Patrick got back, John started calling, asking for money."

"Really? And did Patrick send him any?"

"No, he didn't."

"Why not?" asked Charlotte. "Seeing as he had so much."

"Because John had been left a sizeable inheritance of his own but instead of being careful with it, he'd frittered it away. Patrick said he could see how his spending was getting out of hand when he went to visit. He tried to broach the subject but John would always get argumentative and never wanted to discuss it. Apparently, he'd never been able to keep a job for long so he'd got used to borrowing from his parents for most of his life. Then, when he got his inheritance, he went a bit crazy with it.

"The thing is, Patrick had already given John quite a bit of money during his visit. He couldn't bear to think of him spending everything he had, and ending up with nothing, so he gave him a lump sum and asked him to invest some of it and be careful with the rest. Of course, John blew the lot, didn't he? By the time he got in touch with Patrick, he was really down on his luck. It upset Patrick terribly but he told him he wasn't prepared to give him any more, just so he could waste it, but he *would* be prepared to give him a small allowance every month, instead."

"Aaaww, that was kind of him," said Charlotte.

"Hmpf, John didn't think so. He went berserk, apparently. He couldn't understand why Patrick wouldn't give him what he wanted, seeing as he had so much. He told Patrick he was a selfish so-and-so and to stick his monthly allowance where the sun didn't shine. He said if he ever saw him again, he'd kill him.".

Nathan raised an eyebrow. "Did he now? What his surname Jones as well, do you know?"

Betty's head bobbed up and down. "Yes, I think it was. By the way, just because he said he wanted to kill him, I'm sure he didn't actually do it. For a start, he lives thousands of miles away and, in any case, I doubt he had the money for a flight over here. Anyway, we all say things like that in the heat of the moment but it doesn't mean we're really going to do them, does it? Take me and Ava, for example. If I'd made good on all the times I'd told her I wanted to throttle her, she'd have used up all her lives by now."

Nathan chuckled. "Okay, I think that's all, Betty. I know what a shock this must have been so I appreciate you answering a few questions."

Betty shrugged a shoulder. "Don't mention it. I'm pleased to help. If there's anything I can do, anything at all, please just ask. I'll do whatever I can to help find out what happened to him." Her eyes welled up again. "Sorry, I still can't believe it. He was such a jolly man, always looking forward to doing something or other. I just can't get to grips with this at all. Everyone loved Patrick and he loved life."

"Don't forget, Nathan," said Charlotte, "you were going to ask Betty about Patrick's dentist, remember?"

"Ah, yes. You wouldn't happen to know who it was, would you?"

She shook her head. "I don't think I can ever remember his going to one. He had very good teeth. Not a filling in his head, as I recall. I could be wrong, though.

"You know, I've been praying for something to break the connection between me and Patrick because of that stupid prophecy, but not like this." She reached across the table and clutched Nathan's hand. "You will do your best to find out what happened to him, won't you? And why he disappeared?"

"Who dis'peared?" Molly appeared in the doorway. "Mummy, can we have some blueberries, please?"

"Yes, you can have a few but no more after this, okay? I don't want you all up half the night with tummy aches. And you'll have to take extra care brushing your teeth, okay?"

"'Kay." Molly peered at Betty, who was sniffing and talking quietly to Nathan. "Mummy, why is Betty crying?" she whispered from behind chubby fingers.

"She's had a bit of bad news, love."

"Was it *her* friend what dis'peared?"

"'Who' disappeared, Molly, and yes, it was." Charlotte handed her a bowl. "Now, go on, and don't eat them too quickly."

On her way back upstairs, Molly made a detour. She patted Betty's hand with her little one and said, solemnly, "I'm sorry your friend's dis'peared, Betty. It's sad when that happens, isn't it? Do you remember when Mickey dis'peared? One minute he was there and the next minute, he'd gone." She shook her head and exhaled a sigh, as if the world's most pressing problem was hers to solve. "I cried, didn't I, Mummy? D'you remember?"

Charlotte dropped a kiss on her forehead. "Yes, darling, I do." Neither she nor Nathan had had the heart to break the news that Molly's beloved mouse had gone to the big running wheel in the sky while she'd been at school, so they'd told her he'd run away to the park to be with his mouse friends.

"Anyway, I'd better go. Me and Erin are giving Esme an operation. She fell out of a tree and her guts are all hanging out. It's okay, it's pretend—we're playing hospitals," she said quickly, when Betty's eyebrow shot up, "but we stopped because we got a bit hungry. See you later."

She blew a kiss and dis'peared upstairs to resume surgery.

ooooooo

"Carl, I've got a job for you."

The next morning, Nathan approached one of the new detectives in the team.

"Happy to help, Chief." The enthusiastic young man in the sharp, new suit took the paper Nathan handed him. "What is it?"

"See what you can find out on this guy, will you, please? It's the cousin of our likely John Doe. As he's the only family member we know of, it'd be good to contact him to see if he can tell us anything that might help our enquiries."

"John Jones? That shouldn't take long—must only be a few hundred thousand people in the world called John Jones," Carl joked. "Where does he live?"

"Canada."

"Right. I meant, his address."

"I don't have an address."

"Oh, okay. What province, then?"

"Don't have that either, I'm afraid."

Carl's enthusiasm dipped just a little.

"So you want me to find out what I can about a John Jones who lives in Canada, but we've nothing else to go on?" Carl chuckled. "This is a joke, isn't it? An initiation prank? You know, like sending the new boy out to buy a tin of striped paint and a left-handed screwdriver?"

"If only we had the time for luxuries like pranks," said Nathan. "No, it's a genuine request. All the information we have is on that paper. John Jones is Patrick Jones's cousin. He had another cousin called Lucy, who was Patrick's sister, and an aunt and uncle called Florence and Henry Jones, who were Patrick's parents. He emigrated from the UK to Canada with his parents, more than seventy years ago. More than that, I'd like you to find out and, when you've got any news, let me know asap, okay? Ah, Ben, how did you get on at the bank? Any luck?"

"Actually, the manager was surprisingly helpful." Ben hung his jacket haphazardly on the back of his chair. "There's £27,891.32p in Patrick's account, Chief, and he continued to access it for two months after he left Sunny Days, making withdrawals from cash machines in St. Eves and St. Matlock. The last withdrawal he made was on November 14th, four years ago. Since then, there's been no activity on the account at all, apart from his regular pension payments going in."

"He was accessing his bank account locally for two months after he left the retirement home? So he hadn't gone to live in the country at all? Hmm, that's interesting. Where on earth could he have been between leaving Sunny Days and ending up in the sea? Okay. Fiona, how are you getting on with Patrick's mobile phone number? Anything?"

"Nothing yet but I'm working on it. I'll let you know when I've got any news, Chief."

"Yes, do that, please. The quicker we can wind this investigation up, the better."

CHAPTER EIGHT

"Yes, I'll have a chicken salad, please, but do you think I could have a children's portion? I don't eat a lot. And nothing to drink, thanks. And would it be possible to speak to Charlotte?"

A woman with a mass of flame-red ringlets settled herself at a table on the terrace at Charlotte's Plaice.

"Can I tell her who's asking?" Jess took the menu from the table.

"Yes, my name's Holly Simms. I run the weight loss club at the leisure centre."

"Oh, right. Okay, I'll tell her you're waiting— she shouldn't be long, she's got a few meals to do, and your salad, and then I expect she'll be out."

Jess poked her head through the serving hatch into the kitchen. "You joined a weight loss club?"

Charlotte looked up and gave her a sarcastic grin. "Haha, very funny. Yes, I know I've put on a little weight since the café's been closed, thank you."

"No, I meant the woman from the weight loss club at the leisure centre is outside to see you. She's on table five."

Charlotte stopped chopping and wiped her hands on her apron, peering out through the hatch and onto the terrace.

"To see *me*? What for?"

Sherri Bryan

"I don't know, I didn't ask, but if you hurry up and get those meals out, you can go and find out."

ooooooo

"Hi. Here's your salad." Charlotte placed it on the table with an oil and vinegar set. "Jess said you wanted to speak to me?"

"Yes, I did. I'm sorry to bother you at work but this is all a bit short notice." The woman's dimples made an appearance as she gave Charlotte the benefit of a huge grin and half-stood to shake her hand, indicating that she should join her at the table. "Please, sit down. If you can spare a few minutes, of course."

"I can stop for a while." Charlotte pulled out a chair. "What is it you want to speak to me about?"

"I'm Holly. I run the Weight to Waist club; you might have heard of it? Anyway, my sister is Ellen Anderson—she's one of the managers at Sunny Days retirement complex. We're having a joint open evening tomorrow; for prospective residents of the complex to have a look around and, afterwards, we're bringing them to the leisure centre so they can see what our Senior Waists Club is all about. All Sunny Days residents get a 50% discount, you see.

"Anyway, the chef at Sunny Days was all geared up for the event but his wife went into labour this morning two weeks early, so he's not going to be

Page 128

around. Usually, Ellen would step in and do the catering with her daughter, Jemima, but Jem's been so upset since she heard about that skeleton business, Ellen said she's in no fit state to help out." Holly put a forkful of salad greens into her mouth and chewed methodically. "Sorry about that," she said when she eventually swallowed. "I should have waited until after I'd spoken to you before I ate lunch. I've trained myself to eat slowly since I lost weight, you see, or I'll put it all back on again.

"Anyway, we wondered if there's any chance you'd be able to help out? Ellen asked if I would but I'm not too good at preparing lots of food since I lost weight. It puts too much pressure on me." She speared a chunk of cucumber with her fork but thought twice about putting it in her mouth. "I hated leaving Ellen in the lurch so I said I'd ask around and see if I could find someone to do the catering, and a few people suggested you might be able to help. We only want a finger buffet for twenty people. Nothing too fancy, but tasty, you know the sort of thing, I'm sure." She pushed her ringlets over one shoulder and looked at Charlotte with pleading eyes. "Any chance you could take the job? We'll pay you over the going rate, as it's such short notice."

"Well, it still doesn't give me much time to shop for everything and get it all ready." Charlotte glanced at Holly who was holding her breath. "But I'm not working here tomorrow so it shouldn't be too much of a problem."

Holly let out a huge sigh and put her hands together. "Yay! Thank you so much. And thank goodness. You have no idea what a pickle you're getting us out of." She popped the cucumber into her mouth and proceeded to chew thoroughly.

"Tell you what, when you've finished, pop inside and we can talk a little more," said Charlotte. "Enjoy your lunch."

ooooooo

The following evening, Charlotte and Molly arrived at Sunny Days at just after six-thirty, complete with a buffet for twenty.

"Mummy, who are all those people?" Molly pointed at the crowd milling around the car park, some with shoulder cameras.

"I don't know for sure, sweetie, but off the top of my head, I'd say they're reporters."

"Oh. What's reporters?"

"They're people who tell other people about the news and other interesting stuff."

"What's interesting about Sunny Days?"

Not wanting to get into a discussion with Molly about skeletal remains, Charlotte quickly deflected any further comments. "Come on, we'd better get this food out of the car before the guests arrive or they'll have nothing to eat."

As they walked along the path, a young man was positioned in front of the entrance, just starting a live broadcast.

"Here at the Sunny Days retirement complex, the managers have remained tight-lipped about rumours circulating that the partial skeletal remains found last Sunday are those of a former resident. At this time, I am unable to reveal our source but I have it on good authority that the police are close to making an identification. When I have more information, you'll be the first to hear it. This is Andrew Somerfield, reporting for SE Local News. Back to you in the studio."

"Who's he talking to?" Molly stared over her shoulder as Charlotte pulled her large cool box through the door.

"The people who are watching TV at home. He's a TV reporter and that's a cameraman."

There was no one at the front desk so Charlotte rang the bell. Presently, a man with shoulders like boulders and a tee-shirt that clung to his abs ambled down the stairs, his eyes fixed on his phone, the deftness with which his fingers moved across the touch-screen belying his bulk.

He looked up momentarily, grinning when he saw Charlotte but he quickly dropped the smile when Molly stepped out from behind her.

"Do you work here?" asked Charlotte. "I'm catering for an event."

"Ring the bell." He gave a curt nod towards the counter before pulling on a pair of dark glasses, running his hands over his crew cut and stepping out to face an onslaught of questions from the waiting reporters.

Charlotte rang the bell as she watched them surround him, pushing their microphones under his nose before he got into his van and drove off. After a couple of minutes of waiting, just as she was about to go in search of someone to tell her where to lay out the food, the loud voices of a couple coming down the stairs interrupted the calm of the reception hall.

"You told someone, didn't you? Even after the police asked us not to say anything. For once in your life, why can't you just keep your mouth shut, Ellen!"

"I didn't tell anyone...well, only Holly...and Angie from the hairdressers. I'm sure they wouldn't have said anything, though."

"Oh my God, for crying out loud! Angie from the hairdressers has got a mouth like the Channel Tunnel. And you know what hairdressing salons are like for gossip—they're worse than your cheese and wine evenings with the girls. For heaven's sake, we've got twenty people due to arrive in less than an hour. Can you imagine what they're going to think when they see those reporters hanging around outside? I mean, it's hardly a glowing reference, is it?" They stopped to look out of the window.

"Er, excuse me." Charlotte stood up from the chair in the corner.

Ellen and Cooper spun round on the staircase.

"Oh, sorry, I didn't see you there." Ellen came to greet them, her business smile firmly clicking into place. "Didn't our son-in-law, Gavin, just come down? He should have told us you were here."

"Hmpf," said Cooper. "And why would he do that? I'll tell you why; because there was nothing in it for him, that's why."

Ellen ignored her husband. "You're Charlotte Costello, aren't you? And this must be your little helper?"

"I'm not little. I'm six," said Molly, indignantly, pulling herself up to her full height.

"Yes, I'm doing the catering," said Charlotte. "If you could just tell me where to set the food up, I'll be out of your hair in no time."

"Just a second. Cooper strode towards her, his arm outstretched. "Cooper Anderson, nice to meet you.

Bear with me, please, I feel a change of plan coming on." He turned to his wife.

"Ellen, how about if we start off at the leisure centre and then come here afterwards? We can bring the guests through the back entrance and show them the gardens first. That way, we can avoid the reporters completely."

Ellen nodded. "That's a great idea but it doesn't give us much time to call everyone to let them know." She looked at her watch. "I'll go and start ringing around now—I'll take the first ten on the list, Coop, you can take the rest. Excuse me, won't you," she said to Charlotte. "And thanks so much for helping out."

Cooper smiled at Molly who had retreated behind Charlotte again and was peering up at him with suspicious eyes. "So, could you take the food over to the leisure centre, please?"

Charlotte shrugged. "If that's what you want. I'll just see Holly when I get there, shall I?"

"Yes, but let me pay you first. Do you have an invoice?" asked Cooper. "Great. I won't be a minute."

Charlotte and Molly sat down again. A few minutes passed before Cooper's voice came drifting down the corridor, accompanied by a series of dull thuds.

"Mrs. Costello!" *Thud.* "Mrs. Costello!" *Thud.*
"Could you come here, please? It's the second door on
the right." *Thud.*

She took Molly by the hand and followed the
voice and the instructions. Peeking her head around
the open door, she saw Cooper on the phone.

"Sorry to shout like that but I thought I'd better
start making those calls right away." He held up an
index finger. "Oh, hello, Mr. Ramesh, it's Cooper
Anderson from Sunny Days. Yes, I know. Could you
just hold the line for a moment, please?" He put his
hand over the mouthpiece and handed Charlotte a
handful of notes. "Thank you, you've been very
helpful. And there's a nice tip in there for you for your
trouble."

Charlotte closed the door quietly behind her but
not before she'd seen the open case on the wall with
three darts firmly embedded in the centre of a
dartboard which was covered with a picture of the man
she now knew to be the Cooper's son-in-law, Gavin.

ooooooo

"Hi. I'm Charlotte. I'm doing the catering for an
event that Holly and the Andersons are holding this
evening. The woman in the front lobby told me to come
to this room."

"What? Oh, yeah. I guess so." A woman with
sleek ash-blond hair and make-up so perfectly applied,

she appeared not to be wearing any at all, glanced up
from her phone for a nanosecond and nodded to three
folding tables which had seen far better days.

"You want me to put the food on *those?*"

The young woman threw Charlotte a sour look
before finishing her text. She unfurled her impossibly
long legs from underneath her and slunk across the
room. "This is a leisure centre, you know, not a
restaurant. And, yes, that's where the food has to go.
Holly's just gone to get another table and see if she can
borrow some tablecloths from the cafeteria."

"Okay. We'll wait. I'm Charlotte, by the way,"
she repeated, and stuck out her hand.

Blonde girl took it like she had a bad smell
under her nose. "Tara. Pleasure."

"And I'm Molly. You look like my pretty dolly.
Her name's Tabitha."

"Do I?" Tara gave a narcissistic smile.

"Yes, you do. You know, sometimes, if she's a
bad girl, I twist her head round the other way. That
shows her, alright." Molly grinned.

"Really?" Tara took a step backwards and eyed
Molly with trepidation. "Ah, Holly, thank goodness.
You're back."

Holly put down a table and rubbed a hand
across her flustered face. "Oh my gosh, Charlotte, talk
about Ellen and Coop dropping me in the doodaa at

the last minute! The cafeteria haven't got any spare tablecloths and all I've got in the office are some rolls of crepe paper. Do you think they'll be okay?"

"Tell you what, let me come and have a look and if we can't find anything, you'll have to call your sister and ask her to bring something with her."

Holly put her hands together. "You're a lifesaver. Thanks so much." She looked at her watch. "Come on then, we haven't got long, let's see what we can find. Oh, and Tara, as you're not doing anything, do me a favour and fit another bottle on the water cooler, would you?"

Tara opened her mouth and shut it again before stomping off in a sulk.

"That's my assistant," Holly whispered. "She's fine, once you get to know her, but her parents have treated her like a princess all her life so she's not keen on doing anything that might cause her to put a hair out of place or, God forbid, break a nail. She's been with me for six years—she came straight here from college. Oh, hang on a minute." She scrabbled for a tissue and sneezed repeatedly into it. "Sorry, I've had a cold since this morning." She blew her nose. "And who are you?" she asked Molly, who was following behind, holding on tight to Charlotte's hand.

"Molly. Our names sound the same, don't they?"

"Yes, they do. My mum called me Holly because I was born on Christmas day. Why were you called Molly, do you know?"

"Because that was my nanny's name. She's in heaven now."

"Oh. I'm sorry to hear that." Holly looked embarrassed.

Molly shrugged. "'S'okay. I never knowed her."

Holly unlocked the door to the office. "You'll have to excuse the mess—I share with Tara. You'd never believe it to look at her, but she's incredibly untidy. "

As she opened the door, Molly screwed up her face, her fingers flying to her nose. "Eeeeww. It smells like dog poo in here."

Charlotte, who hadn't wanted to comment, answered Holly's enquiring expression. "Sorry to be blunt but that's exactly what it smells like."

"Oh. Okay. I can't smell a thing with this cold." Holly looked around and picked up a pair of trainers from under Tara's side of the desk. "Oh my God, you're right. That's so disgusting!" Her cheeks flushed and she pushed open a window, setting the dirty trainers outside on the windowsill. "Someone had better clean them later and it won't be me." She picked up a bottle of perfume from the desk and sprayed it liberally in the air. "That better?"

Molly unpinched her nose and sniffed. "Hmm. *That* doesn't smell very nice, either, but it's better than dog poo, isn't it Mummy?"

"Right, now where have I put the key to the cupboard?" Holly shuffled through the papers on the shared desk and gave an exasperated sigh. "You know, it's a wonder I can ever find anything on here. No matter how many times I ask Tara to keep to her side, her stuff always finds its way over here." She pushed a pile of papers, furry toys and numerous other of Tara's personal items across the desk.

"There! At least I can see what I'm doing now. Ah, here they are." She opened the cupboard and took out two rolls of crepe paper. "Do you think these will be alright?"

"Perfect," said Charlotte. "Come on, then. Let's get organized. You're going to have twenty people arriving at any minute!"

ooooooo

"Mummy, did you see those trainers that lady put outside the window?"

"No, I didn't, thank goodness." Charlotte checked Molly's seat belt.

"They were just like Daddy's."

"Were they? But for women, you mean?"

Molly shrugged. "Must be for women with big feet," said Molly. "And that perfume was horrid."

"Yes, it wasn't very nice, was it? I can still taste it in my throat. Ooh, look, there's the ice-cream van. Shall we get something with our tip?"

"Yay! Can I have a blueberry double-scoop, please? With a wafer?"

"You can have whatever you want. Come on, let's see what he's got."

ooooooo

"Well, it's a man in his seventies. And I'd estimate that the body has been in the water for between four and five years, although I'm not sure if I'll ever be able to tell you exactly."

Wendy Myers' lilting Geordie accent filled Nathan's ear.

"Whilst the absence of the feet from a body *could* be an indication of sinister activity pre or post death, there's actually a very simple explanation for it in this case. When a body is in the water for a considerable length of time, it's not unusual for the hands, the feet, or the head, believe it or not, to become detached from the rest of the skeleton, which is what I believe has happened here.

"Now, about his leg. It's the right one and it's four point five centimetres shorter, to be precise. Not that much shorter but, as I said, enough to have given him a limp. There are a couple of historic injuries— breaks to the right thumb and index finger which date back to childhood. More recent are the depressed fractures to what's left of the skull which were caused by blunt force trauma and which, I believe, occurred shortly prior to death, and before he went into the water."

"And which account for the missing bone fragments, I assume?"

"Yes, the fractures would have caused the bones to displace although the natural degeneration of the body in the water would also have contributed to any loose bone fragments becoming detached. There are also a couple of bone spurs on the right shoulder."

"Bone spurs?" snapped Nathan. "You're absolutely sure?"

"Nathan, I think I know a bone spur when I see one."

"Okay, sorry. It's just that Dr. Talbot said that Patrick Jones suffered with them, which is why I asked."

"Well, Dr. Talbot is right."

"Okay. So, I assume the injury which caused the large hole in the skull was the cause of death?"

"Eventually, yes, but here's where it gets interesting. The larger wound is the *second* head injury—possibly caused by a fall from a height. There's another one, which was inflicted first, but which wasn't noticed initially because it was disguised by the larger wound."

"There are *two* head injuries? What caused the first one, can you tell?"

"Blunt force trauma again, but from the angle of the fracture and other characteristics of the wound, I'd be inclined to say that it was caused by a blow while the deceased was standing upright. There's also evidence of similar blows to what remains of the upper jaw, all of which I'd say were sustained *before* the victim died."

"So, there's no question that foul play was involved?"

"Well, the initial smaller head wound would have, at the very least, incapacitated him shortly before death so, yes, my opinion is that foul play was involved. The larger wound, and the other broken bones, are consistent with the body having fallen from a height; for example, if he tumbled off a cliff, or jumped, and fell against the rocks on the way down. As you know, the shoreline's treacherous in parts and it wouldn't be the first time someone's taken a fall from one of the hills or cliffs along the coast—accidentally *or* intentionally."

"Hmm, suicide did cross my mind but according to a good friend of his, that would have been the furthest thing from his mind. And, by all accounts,

Patrick Jones hardly had an enemy in the world—we've spoken to very few people who've had a bad word to say about him.

"On the other hand, he *did* leave at short notice, he *didn't* say any goodbyes and he *didn't* leave a forwarding address. Strange for someone who was so popular."

"Perhaps he was going somewhere and didn't want to be found," said Wendy.

"Hmm, perhaps." Nathan massaged the knotted muscles at the nape of his neck. "Any idea what may have caused the initial injury to the skull?"

"All I can tell you at the moment is that it was a heavy object which was used with considerable force. I've still got some tests to carry out, though, so I should be able to tell you more in a few days. Until then, one thing I can say for sure is that, from the look of these wounds, they were inflicted with a fair bit of malice. Someone wanted him dead, without any doubt." She sighed. "What drives some people to do things like this, I'll never know."

"Okay, thanks for the info. And Wendy..."

"Yeah, yeah, Nathan—I'll fast-track it."

oooooo

"Hi." Nathan tucked the phone between his shoulder and his ear as he answered a call and opened the window at the same time. "Hang on...God, it's stifling in here. Ah, that's better. Sorry, you were saying?"

"I asked if you could spare me a minute."

"Yep, I've got a briefing in ten minutes but I'm all yours till then."

"I've been thinking," said Charlotte.

"Oh dear, that's always dangerous."

"Haha, very funny. No, listen, I've been thinking that Fred Bainbridge, the guy I told you about who was responsible for Patrick's sister's death, might have had something to do with his disappearance. Remember I told you what that guy in the pub said? About Fred taking exception to Patrick giving him a battering and threatening to get his revenge, no matter how long it took?"

"Right. He'd be around eighty now, though, wouldn't he? Which means that when Patrick went missing, he'd have been in his late seventies."

"Yes. So? What's age got to do with bearing a grudge? Revenge drives people to do all kinds of things, regardless of how old they are. And anyway, if you need any proof of what people who are approaching their eighties are capable of, just take a look at all the people we know who are in their mid to late seventies—some of them have got more energy than you and me put together."

"Hmm, fair point. Okay, let me just get a pen. Right, Fred Bainbridge, you said, didn't you? Sutton's Folly. Okay, it's worth checking out. Yeah, thanks. I'll see you later."

He strode to his office door. "Amanda, see what you can find out about this guy, will you, please? I want to know where he is, where he's been, what he's been up to, everything you can find out about him."

"Will do. Who is it?"

"It's the man who was responsible for the death of Patrick Jones' sister sixty odd years ago. When he was sent down, he threatened Patrick, apparently. Told him he was going to get his own back and destroy everything he'd ever loved. Something along those lines, anyway. He'll be no spring chicken now but resentments run deep and you know how revenge can drive people for years."

"Only too well, I'm afraid, Chief. Okay, leave it with me and I'll see what I can find out."

ooooooo

The front page of the St. Eves' Herald carried a photograph of Patrick Jones, along with the sobering headline;

IS THIS THE IDENTITY OF THE ST. EVES' SKELETON?

Although a formal identification has yet to be made, skeletal remains pulled from the sea, just off the

St. Eves' coastline nine days ago, are rumoured to be those of Patrick Jones, a former resident of Sunny Days retirement complex in St. Eves, our sources tell us.

Mr. Jones resided at the home until four years ago when he left suddenly, leaving no forwarding address. The owner of the home, Mr. Cooper Anderson gave this brief statement:

"It is with much sadness that myself, and my family, learned of this terrible news. Patrick was an extremely popular member of our small community and news of his passing has affected us all greatly. We are all devastated that we were not able to say goodbye to him, as he left suddenly and without any prior warning. We shall miss him terribly."

If anyone recalls seeing Mr. Jones after he left Sunny Days, or has any information which could help police to establish what may have happened to him subsequently, please contact them on 070 123 321. All information will be treated in the strictest confidence.

Gavin Campbell tossed the newspaper onto the kitchen table and picked the remnants of a bacon sandwich from his teeth. "You seen this? Nice to actually see it in print—makes for very pleasing reading," he crowed to Jemima as she padded into the kitchen, a towel wrapped around her head.

"Seen what?" She scanned the front page and promptly burst into tears. "Gavin, you're so *hateful!* Why would you deliberately upset me? You *know* how fond I was of Patrick," she blubbed.

"Yeah, too bloody fond for my liking. Anyway, I haven't got time to hang around, I want to get on the road before the traffic builds up. I've got a list of places to get to today as long as my arm." He nodded to the newspaper. "Enjoy the read, won't you?" He chuckled and slammed the front door behind him.

Jemima read the article slowly before screwing up the page in a tight fist. As she watched Gavin climbing up into his van, she heard the radio come on at full volume, blasting out a tuneless cacophony of sound.

She threw open the window. 'Why couldn't it have been *you*, instead?!" she shouted after him, but her words were swallowed up by the revs from the van's engine as Gavin wheel spun off the drive.

Flinging herself into the chair, she pulled the towel from her hair and ran her fingers though her tangled mane, her mood black and all-consuming.

I wish something would happen to you to take that smug look off your face. Once and for all.

CHAPTER NINE

"Chief, you're going to want to hear this."

Ben jumped up from his chair in the incident room. "I've just had Adrian McAllister from the Wimpole Road dental clinic on the line. He saw Patrick Jones's picture in The Herald yesterday and thought he looked familiar.

"He checked back in his records which show that he saw Patrick as a walk-in patient two months after he left Sunny Days four years ago—that was in the November. He just wanted a check up—said he hadn't been to a dentist for years—so Mr. McAllister looked him over and took an x-ray. Patrick's teeth were in pretty good shape so no work was needed but he called back a few days later to make an appointment for the following week for a scale and polish. That was the last time they saw him. Mr. McAllister's happy to let us have a copy of the x-ray."

"Brilliant!" Nathan punched his fist into his palm. "See if you can get in touch with that forensic dentist guy who always turns things round really quickly. You know the one I mean? And ask him if he can turn this round even quicker."

ooooooo

Five days later, Nathan received the results of a forensic dental examination which confirmed that the skeleton's teeth were a match to Patrick Jones and reported the recent developments in a TV witness appeal.

"Following a forensic dental examination, I can confirm that the skeletal remains retrieved from the sea just off the St. Eves' coast on August 12th are that of former Sunny Days retirement home resident, Patrick Jones.

"The last reported sighting of Mr. Jones was two months after he left Sunny Days, at St. Eves' Wimpole Road Dental Clinic, at approximately half-past eleven on the morning of November 15th, when he left an appointment, appearing to be in good health and good spirits.

"We are keen to speak to anyone who saw Mr. Jones on the day he disappeared, or in the days following. Likewise, if anyone can give us any information concerning his whereabouts after he left Sunny Days retirement home, which may help us to find out what happened to him, we'd like to hear from you.

"You can contact the incident room on 070 123 321, where our officers are waiting to take your calls. You don't have to give your name, and we will have no way of identifying you. Of course, if you prefer, you can call in to St. Eves' police station where you can speak to an officer in person. If you have any concerns about giving information, I hope I will allay them by assuring you that all information we receive will be treated in the strictest of confidence."

ooooooo

In the Sunny Days club house, Nora Tweedie watched Nathan's TV witness appeal and wiped her clammy hands on her skirt.

She reached into her handbag for the newspaper she'd been carrying around with her since The St. Eves' Herald had put Patrick on its front page, and read the story again.

Her usually neatly-filed nails, just long enough to be complemented by pale varnish, had become chewed and ragged since she'd read the news five days previously. For five whole days, she'd been in absolute turmoil as to what she should do for the best.

"Morning, Nora."

As they joined Nora at the table for an early morning hour of catty conversation, Bea Berry and Jocelyn MacLaine were already engrossed in decimating the appearance of a new arrival to the complex.

"Oh, my God, did you see that *hair!*" Bea shook a sugar sachet before tearing off the corner with her teeth. "She must have been under the dryer for a week."

"And that upper lip." Jocelyn belched without covering her mouth or offering an apology. "Looks like a family of caterpillars have taken up residence on it." She stirred her coffee, all the while her beady, spiteful eyes scanning the room for unwitting prey, her lip curled in a permanent sneer.

Bea slurped her tea. "You're not still crying over that, are you?" She nodded to the newspaper on the table."

"No. Just reading it again," said Nora. "The Detective Chief Inspector's just confirmed that the remains are Patrick's. Did you know?"

Jocelyn scanned the front page. "Hmm, we saw it on the TV in reception. What d'you think happened to him?"

Never one to miss the opportunity to gossip about someone who wasn't there to defend himself, Bea said, "Well, you don't end up sleeping with the fishes unless you've done something pretty bad. He obviously had it coming."

"You know, I couldn't agree more," said Jocelyn, always keen to fuel an unfounded rumour. "I always knew there was something shady about that man. You alright, Nora? You're not your usual, chatty self."

Nora made a feeble attempt at a smile and drank the last of her coffee. "Yes, I'm fine, just a bit preoccupied, that's all. In fact, I'm not feeling too good so I think I'll go back to my place and have a lie-down."

"Oh dear, you're not having one of your bilious attacks, are you?" Bea shuffled her chair away.

"No, no, it's nothing like that. I just need a bit of peace and quiet."

"Well, don't forget it's the opening of that new garden centre this afternoon. They're putting on free nibbles, so I heard." Jocelyn patted her large handbag with a smirk and a wink. "I'll be filling this up while I'm there."

With the sound of Bea and Jocelyn's cackles ringing in her ears, Nora pushed out her chair, picked up the newspaper, and headed for the exit, turning left towards the town centre.

After a brisk, twenty-minute walk, she arrived at her destination and headed straight for the front desk.

"Good morning, Madam. How can I help you?"

"I'd like to speak to DCI Costello, please. I think I might know who was involved in whatever happened to Patrick Jones."

oooooooo

"I'm so sorry to bother you, I know you must be terribly busy." Nora met Nathan's eyes across the table. "It's just that Betty Tubbs always spoke very highly of you and I didn't want to see anyone else."

"Don't even give it a thought." Nathan smiled. "What is it you wanted to speak to me about?"

"Well, I'd be grateful if our conversation could remain between us. I should really have come in to see you as soon as I saw the news in The Herald, but I was so worried I didn't know what to do... You see, if word gets out that I've spoken to you, things could get very uncomfortable for me at the retirement complex."

"Oh yes? Why's that then?"

"Well." Nora looked over her shoulder as if she was expecting to see Cooper and Ellen Anderson creeping up behind her. "I think someone at Sunny Days might have been involved in Patrick's disappearance." She took a deep breath and put her palm to her chest as she let it out. "There, I've said it. Thank goodness."

"And why would you think that?"

"Because when Patrick was alive, we were good friends." A sudden gush of tears leaked over her eyelids. "Sorry." She fumbled for a handkerchief. "We were very close, so you'll understand that this is difficult for me to talk about."

"Of course, take your time."

Nora took a sip from the cup of sweet tea that Fiona set down in front of her and settled into her chair. "Patrick and I used to go all over the place together. We'd go out for meals in the evening, out for lunch, for coffee, we'd even go dancing—not that he was very good at it, mind you, with that leg of his. He even used to come to Weight to Waist with me on a Tuesday evening." She burst into tears again.

"It's a weight loss club, Chief," said Fiona, in response to Nathan's inquiring expression. "At the leisure centre."

"Yes, that's the one," said Nora. "Not that Patrick needed to lose any weight, mind you, he just used to come along to keep me company. Anyway, I don't know if you know, but Ellen Anderson's sister, Holly, runs the classes.

"Well, one evening, we got to the class and we'd been waiting for over half an hour and she still hadn't turned up. I mean, to be honest, some weeks I could have done without it, you know, getting on the scales and all that hoo-haa. It wasn't so bad if you'd *lost* weight but if you'd *gained* any—well, Holly would make you feel like a complete failure. She'd do it in such a nice way, though, you didn't realise until afterwards that you felt absolutely awful about yourself. Losing weight isn't easy, you know—it's all too quick to find its way to your hips but it can take forever to get rid of it—especially if you've got a sweet tooth, like me."

"Yes, I can imagine." Nathan leaned on the table, his fingers steepled under his chin. "So, what happened after Holly didn't show up at the class?"

"Oh, yes, sorry, I'm easily distracted. Well, Patrick had gone off for a stroll around the leisure centre, as usual. He rarely stayed in the class with me, you see. He'd go off and look at the notice board and chat with people in the cafeteria to pass the time. Anyway, as he was walking past one of the offices, he heard Holly talking to someone on the phone. He only stopped because he recognised her voice and he knew we were all waiting for her. He was going to knock on the door and tell her to get a move on but, when he heard what she was talking about, he decided it would be far more interesting to listen instead."

"And what *was* she talking about?"

Nora took another sip of her tea. "Don't rush me, I'm getting to that. Now, just over five years ago, there was a nationwide competition between all the clubs to find a Weight to Waist Champion. Whoever lost the most weight in a year, through healthy eating and exercise, would win £150,000."

"Oh, yes, I remember that," said Fiona. "Holly won, didn't she?"

Nora nodded. "She did. She won the big prize. She lost a phenomenal amount of weight so she deserved it. Or so we thought. Anyway, turns out that she'd had some kind of weight loss surgery. You know, one of those band thingies they put on your stomach to make it smaller so you can't eat so much. But there must have been something wrong with hers because when Patrick was listening at the door, he overheard her talking to Ellen. She was saying that she wanted to go back to see her surgeon because her weight loss had stalled and she needed him to adjust the band. Honestly, she was like a twig, she didn't need to lose any more weight, but she'd become obsessed with it. And she was asking Ellen to split the cost of the adjustment procedure with her from her share of the winnings. She said Ellen only had the money because of her so it was only fair she should contribute."

"So Ellen knew that Holly had cheated to win the prize? But she took half the winnings, anyway?" said Fiona.

"So it seems."

"And did Patrick tell anyone else what he'd heard?" asked Nathan.

"No. He was going to but he changed his mind. He decided it would be better to confront her about it instead, and suggest that *she* come clean to everyone about what she'd done herself."

"So did he speak to her after the class?" said Fiona.

"No. He went to her house. He knew where she lived because while the leisure centre was being remodelled, she held the class in her living room. Patrick used to come and pick me up afterwards."

Fiona's brows lifted. "I can't imagine she was impressed with him turning up on her doorstep?"

"No, she wasn't—suffice to say, she didn't invite him in. Anyway, he told her that he knew she'd had weight loss surgery and he thought she should come clean and admit to what she'd done. He told her she was supposed to inspire people to lose weight, not con them."

"I bet that went down well. Not," said Fiona.

"You can say that again. Patrick said they started arguing like mad. He was telling her to own up and she was screaming at him to mind his own business. And then she told him that if he ever breathed a word of what he knew to anyone, she could make Jemima's life very uncomfortable. I've no idea what she meant by that—I mean, she was the girl's aunt, for heaven's sake—but it was enough to make Patrick back off. Everyone knew how much he thought of Jemima."

"Hmm, interesting. I wonder if Ellen Anderson knew that he'd found out?"

"Well, if she did, it wouldn't have been from him—he never said another word about it to anyone—but I'm sure Holly would have told her. Ellen would have been furious to know that Patrick had found out because she has so much at stake. Can you imagine what would have happened to Sunny Days if people found out that she was covering up a huge scam with her sister? She couldn't afford for anything to have tarnished the reputation of the complex, and *that* certainly would have."

"Well, I shall look at Ellen Anderson through different eyes from now on, I can assure you," said Fiona.

"And don't be fooled by Holly, either," said Nora. "That innocent act she puts on—playing nice with everyone. Well, I saw a different side to her after what Patrick told me. I haven't been to a class since." She finished her tea and dabbed at her mouth.

"Anyway, I hope you can understand why I was reluctant to come and talk to you. I could be wrong, but if Patrick's disappearance *was* connected to him finding out about Holly cheating to win that prize, I don't even want to think about what might happen to me if anyone finds out that I know about it too."

"Well, I can assure you, Mrs. Tweedie, everything you've told us is in the strictest confidence."

"Thank you, that's very reassuring." Nora placed a hand on Nathan's arm. "You will find who did this to Patrick, won't you?"

"That's the plan. Believe me, we'll do everything we can."

ooooooo

"Didn't you say that Charlotte did a catering job for Holly Simms, Chief?"

"Yes, a few days ago. She said she was a very pleasant woman. If what Nora said is true, it just goes to show how people can hide their true characters when they want something from you."

"When are we going to question her?"

Nathan's assistant, Amanda, poked her head around the door. "Jemima Campbell just called. Asked if I could pass her message onto the DCI or DS Farrell. Said she's got something for you which might help the investigation."

"Okay. What's she got?"

"She didn't want to give any info over the phone—asked if you could call round to see her. She's not working today so she's at home."

"Right then, come on, Fiona." Nathan picked up his keys and phone. "No time like the present. We'll call round to see her now and then we'll pay Holly Simms a visit."

"Sounds like a plan. I'll get my jacket."

ooooooo

"I'm very interested to find out what it is she's got that she couldn't tell us about before." Nathan shrugged on his jacket as he and Fiona walked up the path to Gavin and Jemima's modest staff cottage in the grounds of the retirement complex.

"Who knows? But there seem to be lots of secrets around this place so it could be anything." Fiona lowered her voice as a silhouette approached the other side of the front door.

"Good morning, Mrs. Campbell. We're here in connection with your call."

"Come in. I've got a virus so you'll excuse me if I don't offer to make tea or be the perfect hostess." Jemima flopped listlessly onto the couch. "Mind you, even if I wasn't feeling rough, I think I'd have been tempted to give work a miss today. I'm not sure how much longer I can cope with running the reporter gauntlet, especially not after the recent news. I've had enough of microphones being shoved in my face and people wanting to know about Patrick."

"Yes, it must be difficult." Fiona sympathised. "Which is why it's great that you've got something for us that might help us find out what happened to him."

"I hope so." Jemima heaved herself up from the couch and walked lethargically to the bookcase.

"Is your husband here, by the way?"

"No, not at the moment." Jemima began removing books from a low shelf. "I don't know where he is, actually. I haven't seen him since yesterday lunchtime."

"What, not at all?" said Nathan.

"No. He had appointments all afternoon and then he, er, must have stayed in a hotel, or somewhere, rather than drive back too late. He might have popped in this morning, on his way to work but if he did, I didn't see him because I didn't wake up until ten." She reached to the back of the shelf and pulled out a large paper bag.

"That looks interesting," said Nathan. "I can't wait to find out what it is."

"Well, before I tell you, I have a confession to make." Jemima sank back down on the couch. "I know I should have told you this before, but I kept some of Patrick's things. No one else knows and I know I probably shouldn't have, but I wanted something of his to keep."

"If you don't mind me saying, that's rather an obvious hiding place," said Fiona. "Bearing in mind your husband's dislike of Mr. Jones, are you not worried that he might find it?"

"Huh, you must be joking. This is the safest hiding place in the house because Gavin's never read a book in his life. I don't think he's ever looked at the bookcase, let alone taken anything off the shelves. He's more interested in magazines with pictures...if you know what I mean."

She removed the contents of the bag. "There isn't much; a silver sixpence that was in one of his jacket pockets. It must be a dud—it hasn't brought me much luck yet." She managed to raise a smile. "And this scarf, which I thought would be a nice thing to keep because it's got a monogram of his initials on it. And then there's this book." She flipped through the pages of a copy of Treasure Island and a slip of paper fluttered to the floor.

"Oh, what's this? I didn't even know it was in there." She bent to pick it up. "I just took the book and put it straight in the bag. I've never even read it—not my thing, really, Nicholas Sparks and J. K. Rowling are more my style. I only wanted it because Patrick left it behind and it was an easy thing to keep."

She handed the slip of paper to Nathan who peered at the faded print. "It's a ticket for the pawnbrokers in the high street." He gave a low whistle. "He sold an 18 carat gold and diamond ring and a watch for over fifty grand."

"A gold and diamond ring?" A furrow pleated Jemima's brow. "He used to wear a gold signet ring with a diamond in it. And a watch with diamonds around the face. Wonder why he sold them?"

"Hmm, this ticket is dated the day before he left Sunny Days," said Fiona. "Didn't you say that the last time you saw him, he was hiding an envelope inside his jacket? And that his behaviour was unusual?"

"Um, yes. It was. And yeah, he did have an envelope inside his jacket. You think it might have had the money from the pawn shop in it?"

"Jemima, we'd like to take all this," said Fiona.

"Do you think it'll help you find out what happened?"

"No guarantees, but it might,"

Jemima handed over the bag. "Then you'd better take it."

ooooooo

Gideon Bartholomew checked his platinum blond quiff in the shopfront window of Kudos Pawnbrokers before peering at the faded ticket through the evidence bag Nathan was holding up.

"Oh, right, yeah. I don't remember *everything* that comes through the doors but I always remember the unusual stuff, and the stuff that stands to make us a lot of money. And I remember this because the watch was fabulous and the ring was even better. And because the guy was in here for *ages*. He was really upset about selling them—he kept taking them off and then putting them on again. Went on like that for ages. Must have had sentimental value, I suppose. Anyway, I left him alone in the end to make up his mind. I suggested that he pawn them instead, if he didn't want to part with them permanently, but he didn't want to. Said he had to sell them because he was going away and wasn't coming back.

"They weren't the first things we'd bought from him, mind you—he'd brought in a few items over the years. Beautiful they were; all 18 carat gold rings, all with diamonds. Not as big as this one, but very special all the same." He ran a hand over his precisely moulded, brilliantined quiff. "Why're you asking about them?" he asked, with casual interest.

"Just making enquiries as part of an investigation. You keep records going back that far?"

"Yep, and since we got our new computer system, I'll be able to find them in a minute or so. Just a sec." Gideon ran his long fingers over his keyboard with lightning speed. "You know his name? Not to worry if not, I'll just search for 18 carat gold instead.

"It's Patrick Jones."

"Okay. Right, yep, here we are. He brought in eight rings, this one included, over...let's see, yes, over a period of three years. All in all, we paid out one hundred and ninety six thousand, eight hundred and sixty pounds to your man."

"Wow, that's serious money. I don't suppose he happened to mention where he was going, did he?" asked Nathan.

Gideon shook his head. "If he did, I don't recall. I just remember him saying that he wouldn't be coming back."

The doorbell rang and he buzzed a client in.

"Anything else I can help you with?"

"Not for now. We'll be in touch if you can." Nathan slipped a card across the desk. "But if you remember anything else in the meantime, give me a call, will you?"

oooooooo

"You know, the more we find out, the more I think this is about money. I reckon someone knew that Patrick had a lot of it and killed him for it. The thing is, if that's the case, why wouldn't they have got him to clear out his bank account before they did the deed?"

"I wish I knew," said Nathan. "Right, let's get this stuff to forensics. I don't know if any of it'll be any good after all this time but if Patrick was killed by someone who knew him, there might be some other DNA on here that'll point us in their direction."

CHAPTER TEN

The opening of any business in St. Eves was always well attended by the community, and the much-anticipated opening of the new garden centre, Blooming Beautiful, was no exception.

As the crowd grew impatient for the Mayor to cut the red ribbon and declare the garden centre open for business, fat bees buzzed lazily amongst rainbow-coloured petals, drunk on their fill of sweet nectar, and butterflies flitted and congregated around lofty hollyhocks.

"This is just what you need to help take your mind off that horrid Patrick Jones business," Harriett said to Betty. "A lovely summer's afternoon surrounded by flowers."

"Yes, I've been looking forward to it. And you're right about flowers—there's definitely something healing about them."

"Oh, for heaven's sake, I do wish they'd get a move on." Ava pushed up the back of her bob, its pastel-pink hue now just a faded memory. "I didn't get a chance to break these sandals in and they're killing my heels."

Betty swerved to avoid a bee. "Broken in or not, they're ridiculous shoes to wear to the opening of a garden centre, Ava. They'll be full of gravel in no time and you'll be hobbling around like a geriatric jogger."

She held out a foot, clad in a bright yellow shoe more befitting the occasion. "What you need are some flat, sensible shoes, like these. I hardly know I've got them on, they're so comfortable."

Ava cast her eyes downward and raised a doubtful brow. "Yes, dear, they're comfortable because they look like they're made of sponge. Each to their own, Betty, but you wouldn't catch me dead in a pair of those. They look like something my great-great-grandmother's grandmother would have turned her nose up at because they were too frumpy."

Betty opened her mouth to retort but instead, found herself stumbling backwards when a man in the crowd stepped back and bumped into her. She let out a small shriek and he turned and grabbed her arms just in time to stop her from falling to the ground.

"Oh, I'm so sorry. How clumsy of me. Are you alright?"

Betty found herself looking at her reflection in his mirrored sunglasses. "Yes, I'm fine, I'm fine. No need to fuss—no damage done."

"Why don't you look where you're going?" Ava scolded. "She could have had a nasty fall."

"But I didn't, did I?" Betty gave the man an amiable smile. "Because this gentleman caught me. Thank you."

"Don't mention it." The man returned the smile and made his way through the crowd to the exit.

"Where's he going?" said Ava. "He's going to miss the opening."

"He must have got fed up of waiting," said Betty.

"I know the feeling." Ava shifted from one foot to the other. "Although we've all wasted at least an hour of our lives standing here, he might as well have waited a bit longer."

"Sshhhh!" Harriett dug an elbow in Ava's ribs. "The Mayor's about to say something."

"About bloody time," she muttered.

"Testing, testing, one, two, three...can everyone hear me? Yes? Right..."

The Mayor, Councillor Arthur Newell, was resplendent in his robes and chains, albeit a little pink around the jowls due to the heat of the day.

"I'll make this short as I know you're all keen to have a good look around." He wiped a bead of sweat from the end of his nose and swatted at the bee which had left Betty in peace and was now dive-bombing his bicorn.

"Thank you all for turning out today to the opening of Blooming Beautiful. It's high time we had a dedicated garden centre in St. Eves so I'm delighted to have been given the honour of officiating at the opening." He dabbed at his increasingly glowing face with a handkerchief of gargantuan proportions, handed to him by his wife, standing a discreet distance behind. "The proprietors, Stuart and Leanne, have asked me to let you know that, for today and tomorrow only, they'll be offering you all a voucher for a 50% discount on everything you buy so, please, dig deep and buy plenty."

He puffed and blew and fiddled with his collar. "I think that's everything covered, so, without further ado, it gives me great pleasure to declare St. Eves' new garden centre, Blooming Beautiful, open for business!"

Amidst cheers and applause, the Mayor cut the ribbon and posed for photos before ducking into the shade of a nearby bamboo gazebo.

As shoppers and browsers surged forward and Ava and Betty wandered off to ooh and aah over the rose bushes, Harriett and Charlotte broke away from the crowd and headed straight for the produce garden; a section dedicated to all things culinary.

"Right." Charlotte took a list from her handbag. "I'm on the lookout for tomato plants, fennel, French beans and some rhubarb. Oh, and some herbs and edible flowers to keep in a window box at the café." She strolled up and down the aisles, waving away a wasp that buzzed past her nose.

Sherri Bryan

"They've got some wonderful things, haven't they?" Harriett picked up a Japanese plum tree, raising her eyebrows at the price ticket before putting it down again. "We'd better get in quick before all the bargains are gone. You know, I'd love a lemon tree if they have any. Some of our friends have one and the flowers are beautiful. They bloom all year round, you know. You have to bring them inside during the winter but it would sit quite happily in the corner of the conservatory in the colder months. The smell of lemons always reminds me of holidays in the Med. We had one outside our hotel when we went to Italy and the perfume was absolutely divine."

"Yes, isn't it? We had a big one in the garden at our house in Spain," Charlotte recalled as she walked down the rows of produce-laden benches. "Mum used to make jars and jars of marmalade from it. There was so much fruit. It seemed like every time you picked a lemon, two grew in its place. Ooh, look, they've got olive trees and banana palms over there."

She marched off to take a better look, stopping when she spied a piece of paper on the ground. She bent to read the writing on it.

"Here, Harriett, listen to this. "'I know something about you that you wouldn't want anyone else to know. Meet me at the new garden centre tonight at 11.00—at the back behind the vegetable

Page 170

section. And you'd better come alone, or your dirty little secret will be out.'" She pulled a face. "Wow, someone obviously wasn't very happy when they wrote this."

"Hmmm, I wonder who it's to? Someone who works here, do you think? Maybe it fell out of their pocket." Harriett scanned the area half-heartedly, looking for likely candidates. "Anyway, what was I saying? Ah, yes, I'm surprised you don't have a lemon tree outside the café. I'm sure you'd use them all the time. I haven't seen one yet, perhaps they're over there in that section where you aaaaaghh!"

"Oh, Harriett! Be careful! Are you okay?" Charlotte rushed back to help her up from where she was spread-eagled on the crazy-paving path.

"Yes, yes, I'm fine." Harriett scrambled to her feet, smoothing her strawberry-blond waves back into place. "No need to fuss. I just tripped over something. What on earth..." Her hands flew to her mouth. "Oh, my goodness, Charlotte! Help! Someone, heeeeelp!"

Sticking out from the middle of a row of banana palms was a pair of large feet, clad in scuffed combat boots.

Breaking off from serving a line of happy customers, Stuart Davidson ran to the scene of the commotion and crouched to the floor to feel for a pulse.

"Is he alright?" Charlotte asked, unable to keep the doubt from her voice.

As a crowd gathered round, Stuart shook his head, confirming that Gavin Campbell had breathed his last.

ooooooo

"Alright, I'll tell him. Thanks."

Fiona turned up the air conditioning and angled the air vent to blow in her face. "That was Amanda, Chief. She said that Frederick Bainbridge, the man who was involved in the death of Patrick Jones' sister that you asked for a check on, passed away three months ago at a hospice in Blastonbury. He'd been terminally ill and his son and daughter-in-law had been caring for him for the past six years until he moved to the hospice five months ago."

"Oh, okay. Well, I'm sorry to hear that, although at least we can exclude him as a person of interest now. If he'd needed care for the past six years, I'd say it's unlikely that he had anything to do with Patrick's disappearance."

"Hmm, unlike Gavin Campbell who I was convinced *was* involved," said Fiona. "PC Milton said something about the body being covered in stings."

They pulled up outside Blooming Beautiful, close to where a crowd of customers who'd been removed from a cordoned-off area were giving statements and grumbling that by the time the garden centre would be open for business again, their 50% discount vouchers would have expired.

"That's Gavin's van parked over there, Chief," said Fiona. "I'll get it cordoned off and let forensics know, and then I'll be in."

As his footsteps crunched over the gravel drive, Nathan heard an all too familiar voice chatting with a police constable. His wife's ability to always be in the wrong place at the wrong time never failed to amaze him and he shook his head as she waved, a sheepish expression on her face.

"Yes, of course I know how you feel about me getting involved in police business but it's not like I was *trying* to get involved," she explained, as Nathan's eyebrows lifted higher and higher. "I just *happened* to be here for the opening and just *happened* to find the note on the ground before Harriett tripped over that poor guy's feet. I don't know why you find that so hard to believe."

The corners of Nathan's mouth twitched. "Charlotte, whenever something suspicious happens, you have an uncanny knack of being in the vicinity."

She opened her mouth to respond, her expression beyond indignant. "I don't go looking for dead people, you know. They just seem to crop up with alarming regularity these days."

Nathan scratched his chin. "Hmmm, you have a point."

"I'm just glad that Molly wasn't here to see it—thank goodness she's spending the day with Esme and Erin." Charlotte glanced over to the outdoor café where Harriett was retelling her story to Ava and Betty. She lowered her voice. "What happened to him, do you think? The garden centre owner said it looked like he was covered in wasp stings."

Nathan shrugged. "I've no idea, but I'm sure we'll find out soon enough. Look, I'll speak to you later. I don't know what time I'll be home so give Molly a kiss from me if I don't see her before she goes to bed."

"Okay, see you later."

ooooooo

"I've told you, we've been here since the crack of dawn; me, Leanne, and the others, and none of us saw that body."

Stuart Davidson, the owner of Blooming Beautiful, ran his soil-stained fingers down his perspiring face.

"Look, obviously, we would have called the police if we had—we wouldn't have just left him there, would we? I mean, it's not exactly what we were hoping for on our open day—a customer tripping over a dead body in the middle of the Exotic Trees section. Talk about a downer." Stuart slumped on the end of a bench and put his heavy head in his hands. "I'm just glad it's no one I recognise. We've had people stopping by all week; coming in and looking around, asking us how we were getting on and if we'd be ready to open in time, but I don't remember him."

Fiona flipped a page in her notebook. "What I don't understand, Mr. Davidson, is how the body must have been lying here all morning without anyone seeing it. You say you've all been here since very early so how was it not noticed?"

Stuart shrugged. "I dunno. The trees don't need a lot of fussing and they'd all been watered last night so we didn't bother with them today. There was no need, see? All we did this morning was put out all the herbs and fruit and veg plants on the benches. I don't know how no one saw him but they obviously didn't. We've all been pretty preoccupied, you know."

"But you're sure it was already here when you opened up this morning?"

Stuart contemplated the question. "Yeah, it must have been. It definitely wasn't here yesterday while we were getting set up so it must have turned up after we left here at around eight and before we got back this morning at seven. I saw the note that woman found by the body, by the way. It said that someone wanted to meet him here last night at 11pm but, if that was the case, I don't understand the stings. They look like wasp stings because there's no barb left in the skin, but wasps don't come out at night. I don't get it."

Fiona nodded. "Well, I can assure you, we'll make it our business to find out what happened as soon as we can. And it would help us a great deal if all your employees would agree to give a handwriting sample, and their fingerprints—it'll help to eliminate them from our enquiries."

"Well, I'm sure that won't be a problem but I guarantee that note won't have been written by anyone who works here," Stuart said, with indignation. "I've known them all for years and I'd bet my life that none of them are responsible."

"DS Farrell! Sorry to interrupt." One of the SOCO team beckoned to Fiona from the cordoned off area across the other side of the garden centre. He held out an evidence bag containing a cardboard box with several holes pierced in the lid. "It's got what appears to be paté and insect droppings inside. And it looks like someone's left a partial print in the paté."

"Well, that's great news. And very interesting about the insect droppings. Okay, thanks for letting me know." She went back to where Stuart was craning his neck, trying to hear.

"What's going on? Have you found a clue?"

"Hopefully." Fiona smiled. "Thank you for your time, Mr. Davidson."

They made their way over to where Nathan was just finishing up his conversation with Leanne Davidson.

"I know it's easy at the moment for people to just walk in off the street when there's no one here," said Leanne, "but the company who were supposed to fit the gates let us down yesterday at the last minute. We didn't want to delay opening so we decided to go ahead. We weren't too concerned about having to wait for them for a few days, because we can lock stuff in the office temporarily, but we had no idea that someone would have the place earmarked for something like this." She twisted her ponytail around her finger distractedly. "It's awful. That poor man."

Leanne gave her husband a hug and they went off, hand in hand.

"You waiting for me, Fiona?"

"Yes, Chief. Just wanted to let you know that SOCO have made an interesting find which backs up Stuart Davidson's theory that Gavin Campbell might have been killed by wasp stings. Looks like someone brought them here in a box smeared with paté of some description which, fortunately for us, they've left a partial print in. I know it's too early to say if that's what killed him but it's a bit of a puzzle because, apparently..."

"Wasps don't come out at night." Nathan finished her sentence.

"Exactly."

ooooooo

"We're so sorry for your loss." Fiona sat in front of Jemima for the second time that day.

Jemima shook her head.

"She can't speak. Can't we do this another time?" Ellen Anderson's eyes were like slits in a piece of beef as she comforted her daughter.

"No, Mum, it's okay. I've got to speak to them sooner or later and I'd rather get it over with." She wiped her eyes, wrinkling the delicate skin beneath them with a dry tissue. "Did you know he was allergic to insect bites and stings? He was supposed to carry one of those pens to inject himself with but he always left it in the van." She sighed and wiped her eyes again.

"If you need to stop at any time, just say the word, okay?" said Fiona. "Now, you told us earlier that you hadn't seen your husband since yesterday. That's right, isn't it?"

"Yes. Not since yesterday, around lunchtime."

"And you weren't concerned when he didn't come home?"

Jemima's laugh was humourless. "Not really. Gavin didn't come home lots of nights."

"Do you know where he might have been?"

"Well, I couldn't say for sure," said Jemima, "but, if I had to guess, I'd say he was with a woman."

"I see. Do you know who?"

"I've no idea, and I didn't want to know, although I doubt there was only one. It was bad enough that, on the nights he *did* come home, more often than not he'd stink to high heaven of someone else's sickly-sweet perfume."

"Jemima, you're in shock. You don't know what you're saying." Ellen grabbed her hand. "Gavin could have easily picked up the smell of another woman's perfume in the pub, or the leisure centre."

"Oh, Mum, please don't try to make excuses for him any more. He doesn't need them now."

"Jem, you're upset. This is your *husband* you're talking about. Honestly, the poor man came home late a few nights and you immediately accuse him of being a serial adulterer." She tapped her head. "It's all in your mind, love."

"Oh, yeah, of course. All in the mind. You mean like the makeup on his shirts?" Jemima wiped a tissue across her face and looked Nathan straight in the eye. "The reason Gavin felt the need to spread himself about is because he felt inadequate. He'd been on steroids for so long, they'd made him infertile. He'd wanted children ever since we got married but we couldn't have them and he couldn't stand that he'd failed at something. In the end, he wasn't even interested in me. He just went elsewhere for his jollies. *That's* why he was seeing other women for years."

Ellen gasped. "Jemima! For heaven's sake!"

"Mum, why are you *still* sticking up for him?! He's dead—you don't have to any more." Jemima staggered from the couch to the window. "Anyone would think *he* was your blood relative and I was the in-law," she mumbled.

"Jem, that's a dreadful thing to say! The only reason I stuck up for Gavin was because your father and Paul treated him so badly. I've no idea why, but they were so rude to him. I just wanted to be nice. Is that such a bad thing?"

Jemima shook her head. "No, Mum, it's not. It's just that sometimes, it felt like you were nicer to him than you were to me." She sighed. "You know when I think back to the first year we were married..." She bit her lip and shook herself out of her reminiscing. "Anyway, now you know, that's why he used to see other women. And why I just let him get on with it. I couldn't cope with all the self-pity and the 'woe is me' so, in the end, I decided that someone else could listen to it. I'd had enough. In fact, I've had enough now. I'm too weak to talk to you anymore. I'm sorry."

Nathan stood up to leave. "Don't worry. We'll be back in touch if we need to speak to you again."

The door opened and Cooper Anderson burst into the room. "Jemima! I was at the bank—I've only just heard. Oh, my darling, I'm so sorry." He pulled his daughter into a hug and threw a glare at Nathan and Fiona. "Can't you leave her alone? She's just lost her husband, for God's sake."

"Actually, we've already spoken to Mrs. Campbell. She was very co-operative. We were just about to leave and come up to the office—we'd also like to have a quick word with you and your son before we leave, if that's convenient?"

Cooper gave a curt nod. "I suppose so. If you go on, I'll be there in a few minutes. Paul's there already so I'll call him when I get there."

oooooooo

"Hello."

"Hi, it's me. Can you talk?"

"Yes. Quite well, actually. I've been doing it for years."

"Ha, very droll. Have you got a minute?"

"Yes, I'm at Sunny Days with Fiona."

"Ah, that's good. I didn't think to mention it until just now but when Molly and I went there the other day, I saw a dartboard in Cooper Anderson's office."

"That's very interesting, Charlotte. Would you like me to speak to him about organising a darts-themed social evening? Andersons vs Costellos?"

"Don't be facetious, Nathan. No, I was calling to tell you that it had a picture of Gavin Campbell in the middle and Cooper was throwing darts at it."

"Was he, indeed?"

"Yes. I completely forgot about it until just now."

"Well, that's very interesting. Thanks."

"Okay, see you later."

oooooooo

"What do you want to talk to *me* for?"

"For heaven's sake, Paul!" Cooper Anderson spluttered. "Gavin's just been found dead at the opening of that new garden centre. Why do you *think* they want to talk to you?"

"We're talking to all Gavin's family members, not just you," said Fiona.

"Hmpf, he wasn't any family of mine." Paul scoffed at the very notion.

"You didn't get on?"

"No, we didn't. I couldn't stand him. He treated Jemima like...well, he treated her really badly. She should never have married him."

"Your mum said you're very protective of your sister. Is that right?"

"Yeah, I suppose I am. I always look out for her." He slouched in his chair but sat upright when he'd considered the implications of Nathan's words.

"Oh, I see what you're doing. You're trying to imply that I had something to do with this? Well, I might be protective of Jem but I didn't kill her husband. God! What d'you take me for. I'm studying to be a marine biologist, not a flippin' serial killer."

"I wasn't "trying to imply" anything of the kind. I was simply asking about your relationship with your sister," said Nathan, his voice calm in contrast to Paul's manic one.

"In any case," said Paul. "I wasn't even here when his body was found, so I can't have done it, can I?"

"He probably wasn't murdered today," said Cooper.

"Well, whenever it was, it was nothing to do with me." Paul chewed on a thumbnail and stared out of the window. "Can I go now?"

"Yes, you can go," said Fiona. "For now."

Paul jumped up from the chair and left the room without a word to anyone.

Cooper ran a hand through his tousled hair. "I just can't take this in. I was only speaking to Gavin yesterday. And I was cursing him this morning because he wasn't around to go to the wholesalers, so I had to go and it made me late for my appointment at the bank. I just can't get my head around it."

"Mr. Anderson. That case on the wall." Nathan pointed to the dartboard.

"Sorry?"

"That case. Could you open it, please?"

Cooper's forced laugh couldn't disguise his unease. "It's just a dartboard."

"Yes, I thought it was. But could you open it, please?"

Cooper hesitated. "I'd rather not," he mumbled.

"Why's that? It's just a dartboard, after all."

"Your wife told you, didn't she?" Cooper smacked his palm on the desk. "She must have seen it the other day when she came in here."

"Mr. Anderson, it would be much easier if you just opened the case, please."

Cooper sighed and opened the case to reveal a well-dented, close up picture of Gavin's face.

"I know how this must look," he said, "but you have to believe that I had nothing to do with his death. I just couldn't stand the way he treated Jemima, and Ellen won't hear a bad word against him so the only way I could vent my frustration was on that dartboard." He looked at Nathan. "You've got a daughter, haven't you? How would *you* feel if you knew someone was treating her badly? Wouldn't *you* want to kill them? Not that I did, mind you, I'm just making a point."

Nathan stared at him for a while, then nodded. "Okay, Mr. Anderson. That's all for now but please don't go anywhere too far. Until we find out who was responsible for your son-in-law's death, I'm sure we'll be seeing quite a lot of each other.

CHAPTER ELEVEN

"Mummy, will I be able to have my nails painted?"

"Yes, darling, but only with pale-pink or clear varnish. Nothing too dark, okay?"

"And my toenails, too?"

"Yes. We're all having a mani-pedi."

"And can I go in that bubble bath thingy?"

"You mean the hot tub? Course you can, if you want to."

"Wheeeeee!" Molly pumped her arms up as she skipped along next to Charlotte. "I'm sooo excited! I can't wait!"

Charlotte and Molly were on their way to keep a date at St. Eves' only five star hotel, where an eagerly anticipated spa morning with Sharon Donovan and her twin girls, Erin and Esme, awaited, followed by lunch on the rooftop terrace with its pool and spectacular views across St. Eves.

"Good morning, Madam, Miss." An enthusiastic meeter-greeter with a smile as wide as a frisbee, pounced as soon as they exited the revolving door into the lobby of the President Hotel. "Are you here for the Mother and Children Pamper Package?"

"Yes, we are," answered Molly. "And I'm having my toenails painted and everything!"

"Well, you're a very lucky girl, then." The young woman smiled. "My name's Danielle and I'll be explaining a little bit about what you can expect from your session. Come on, I'll walk you to the lift." She chattered away, extolling the benefits of the treatments, the quality of the products and the qualifications of the therapists.

"Do you have any questions?" she asked when she'd finished.

Molly had already sized the woman up before beginning her inquisition. Her hand shot up in the air. "Yes, I have a question."

"Alrighty. What would you like to know?"

"Have *you* got any children?"

"Molly, that's personal." Accustomed to Molly's grillings, Charlotte raised a warning eyebrow.

Danielle shook her head. "It's okay, I don't mind. No, I don't have any children. Not yet, anyway. I don't really have time at the moment—I'm far too busy with work." She wiggled her ring finger in the air. "And I don't have a husband."

Molly dismissed the very suggestion with a flap of her hand. "Oh, you don't need to have one of *those*— loads of my friends' mummies don't have husbands but they've still managed to have babies okay. Haven't they, Mummy?" She paused for thought. "I'm pretty sure they just popped them out of their belly-buttons."

"Molly, that's enough. Come on, the lift's here. I
can see we need to have a little chat sometime."

The amused meeter-greeter wiped away the
tears as the doors closed. "It's the eleventh floor—enjoy
your morning!"

ooooooo

"I'm so relaxed, I could just drift off to sleep
sitting here in my chair." Sharon Donovan speared a
chunk of lobster tail and dunked it in lemon
mayonnaise. "I'm sure that massage has turned my
bones to jelly."

"Hmmm, it *was* good, wasn't it?" Charlotte
stretched out her legs and admired her pedicure of
bright yellow sunflowers on a background of vivid
orange varnish. "Do you think this is too much?"

"What? No, it looks fab. Very summery." Sharon
tipped her face to the sun. "Aaaah, this is bliss. I'm
glad you could make it. Esme and Erin missed Molly
on their birthdays."

"Yes, sorry about that—my fault. What with
going to Sutton's Folly at the last minute, I completely
forgot." Charlotte checked on the girls who were
giggling and chatting away in the hot tub. "Have you
finished your lunch? We can go and grab a couple of
sun beds if you have. We can relax properly, then, and
keep a closer eye on the girls."

"How *was* Sutton's Folly, by the way? I've hardly seen you since you got back." Sharon fluttered her towel over a bed and waved at a waiter for another mango and kiwi mocktail.

"Oh, you know. It had its ups and downs. Let's just say that I'm glad to be home."

"Well, you certainly got back in time for all the action," said Sharon. "I've been glued to the news on the TV *and* in the papers." She perched on the edge of the sunbed and rubbed lotion into her shoulders. "First that poor old guy's bones were dragged out of the sea and now all this business with Gavin Campbell. It must be an exciting life, being married to the DCI."

"It certainly has its moments," said Charlotte, "although we don't see much of Nathan when he's working on cases like this. Most days, he's out early and back late. I hope they get a break soon. Sometimes it's just one thing that can help bring all the loose ends together. *Molly!* Don't jump about in the hot tub, please! I don't care what you're doing, if you can't sit down, you can come out."

"Did you know Gavin Campbell, by the way?" asked Sharon.

"I met him once, very briefly when I went to Sunny Days to cater for an event. Did you?"

"I only met him a few times but, believe me, that was enough. Charlie knew him, though, from his army days."

"Gavin was in the army?"

Sharon nodded. "Used to be, years ago when he and Jemima first got together, but he got really heavily into weight training and body building."

"I would have thought that was a good thing if you're in the army."

"Well, it probably is, until you test positive for steroids," said Sharon as she slathered lotion onto her shins. "Which is what happened to Gavin during a random drug test and he got booted out. You'd think that would have stopped him taking the flippin' things but it didn't. If you ask me, steroids are at the root of all his and Jemima's problems."

She hugged her knees to her chest. "Anyway, it must have been about a year after he left the army, Charlie and I were at the St. Eves' Tavern one night and Gavin was there with a crowd of people, drinking too much and generally making an idiot of himself." She leaned forward and lowered her voice. "He was telling them about some woman he was seeing. As if poor Jemima didn't have enough to deal with."

"He was having an affair back then?" said Charlotte.

"Yeah. Must be about six years ago, I suppose."

"Do you know who he was seeing?"

"No idea. From what I can gather, there'd been more than one woman over the years but this new one was someone he met when he started going to the leisure centre."

Charlotte's ears pricked up. "Really?"

"Yeah. Anyway, I was saying to Charlie last night, I wouldn't be surprised if a jealous husband had caught up with Gavin eventually. It makes you think if that had something to do with him being bumped off, don't you think?

"Hmmm, it certainly does."

ooooooo

"Hello my little munchkin." Nathan caught Molly in a squeeze and swung her round."

"Daddy, Daddy! Yaaay! You're home early!" Molly threw her arms around his neck and blew a raspberry on his cheek.

"I am, sweetheart, but only for half an hour. I've got to get back to work, but I had to drop in and find out how you enjoyed your morning at the spa because you'll be asleep when I get home later. Did you enjoy it?"

"Oh, Daddy, it was brilliant. We had our nails painted and then a lady rubbed my shoulders while I was lying down on a bed thingy with a hole in it where I had to put my face. It was weird. And then we had pizza and fruit salad and me and Esme and Erin went in the hot tub for *ages*. My fingers were all crinkly when I came out, like the prunes Ava puts on her porridge. I wanted to show you but they went away. See?"

"Not to worry, Mol, I can imagine what they must have looked like." Nathan lay on the rug and wrestled the dogs. "Where's your mum, is she upstairs?"

"No, she's in the garden, planting stuff. Then we're going on a bike ride."

Nathan nodded and wandered into the garden, Pippin and Panda at his heels.

"Hello, what are you doing here? I wasn't expecting you until tonight." Charlotte rubbed the back of her muddy hand across her forehead."

"Just popped home for a while to see my two favourite girls." Nathan took her in his arms. "How was your visit to the spa?"

"Fabulous. I feel like I've got loads more energy. I think I might treat myself more often. Actually, I was going to call you after I'd finished doing this."

"Oh? What for?"

"Because I heard something today that might help your investigation into Gavin Campbell's death."

She recounted the story Sharon had told her.

"So, he started an affair six years ago with someone he met at the leisure centre?"

"Apparently."

"But Sharon doesn't know who?"

"No, but when I was there the other day, Holly happened to mention that Tara, her assistant, had come to work at the centre straight from college, six years ago. Could be a coincidence, but… And then, Molly and I went into the office with Holly and there was a pair of trainers with dog poo on the sole under Tara's side of the desk. *I* didn't notice them—well, I noticed the stench—but Molly said they were like yours. But not for women, they were big, like a man's. Again, could be a coincidence, but I thought you should know."

"Hmm, that's interesting. I'll make a detective of Molly yet."

"Be serious. Anyway, before that, when I was at Sunny Days, I saw Gavin and he was engrossed in texting on his phone. And when I went to the leisure centre five minutes later, Tara was doing exactly the same. I mean, that's not proof that they were seeing each other, of course, but I'm telling you everything in case it's of some use. *And*," she rustled in her handbag and produced a small card, "here's her number. It's on the business card Holly gave me the other day." She read from it. "Tara Frost, her name is."

"Thank you. I'll give this to the guy who's checking Gavin's phone records and see if it's in his call log." Nathan kissed the end of her nose. "As usual, you're a godsend. I'll see you later."

∞∞∞∞∞

Charlotte switched off the TV and went to sit next to Nathan at the dining room table where paperwork and files were strewn across its surface.

"Are you going to be long? I'll wait up for you if not."

"I'll be another hour, or so, I suppose. You go up." He dropped a distracted kiss on the side of her head, catching her on the eye.

"Ow! Your stubble scratched my eyeball."

Nathan threw down the document he was reading and pulled her into a hug. "I'm sorry, love. And I'm sorry to bring work home but with everything that's going on, it's a chance to look through things without getting distracted every five minutes."

"It's okay, I know you've got a lot on your plate. I just don't like it when you stay up all hours and then rush out of the house at the crack of dawn. I know you're busy but you need to sleep too, you know."

She looked down at the table, her gaze falling on Patrick Jones's Sunny Days file and she casually opened it, removing the papers from it and flicking through them while Nathan was occupied with his paperwork.

"Erm, when you've quite finished?" said Nathan, looking up from the table, a wry smile on his lips.

"Oops, caught in the act. Sorry." Charlotte was putting the papers back in the folder when something on the back cover caught her eye. She took it and held it under the light. "How's Carl getting on with tracking down John Jones?"

"Not too well." Nathan stretched his arms up to the ceiling and yawned. "There are almost 5,000 people called John Jones in Canada and we've only got limited information on him so it's not a simple job. I'm sure Carl will come up with something but he's not had much luck so far. Why d'you ask?"

"Because there's a phone number here for him."

"*What?* Where?" Nathan jumped up from his chair.

"Here. See." Charlotte held the folder up to the light and an indentation of a name and phone number became clearly visible. "It must have been there since the note was first made on the file."

"Charlotte, as always, whatever I said about not wanting you to get involved in police business, I take it all back. When I give this number to Carl tomorrow, I think he might cry with relief."

"Well, I hope it'll give you a lead although he might have changed his number since then. Fingers crossed he hasn't, though." She cocked her head to one side. "So, does this mean, as I found you such a *huge* clue, that you'll come up to bed now?"

"Just try and stop me," said Nathan, as he flicked off the light and chased her up the stairs.

CHAPTER TWELVE

"Chief, you got a minute?"

"Yes, come on in, Fiona. What's up?"

"Well, it looks like the Anderson family are pretty good at keeping secrets. I've finally managed to get some details on the calls on Patrick's phone. It took a while because the number doesn't exist any more, and it was so long ago, but the phone provider was really helpful. Anyway, turns out that the last call Patrick made from that number before he left Sunny Days was to *this* number." She held up a piece of paper.

"And who's that registered to?"

"Cooper Anderson."

ooooooo

In Cooper Anderson's office, his confusion was palpable.

"Yes, that number was registered to me but it wasn't *actually* mine. It was Paul's. I just paid for it while he was at school."

"This number belonged to your son?"

"Yes, but it was just a temporary number for a basic phone. We only gave it to him in case of emergencies. He got rid of it when he was sixteen and got a smartphone with a new number. Why? Is there a problem?" He rubbed at the crease in his forehead

"I hope not," said Fiona. "Where is Paul, Mr. Anderson, do you know?"

"He's on his way to a friend's birthday party on the beach—at the Hula-Hula bar. You've only just missed him but he's going into town first to meet up with some friends and going on from there. He probably won't be there for half an hour, or so. I'll call him, shall I?" Cooper picked up his phone.

"No, it's okay, thank you. We'd prefer to speak to him ourselves. Thank you for the information."

ooooooo

"The Anderson family never fail to surprise, do they, Chief?"

"You're not wrong there, Fiona." Nathan negotiated the lunchtime traffic, turning left onto the seafront.

"Actually, sorry to be a pain, but is there any chance we could stop off at the station on the way? I've got the start of a migraine and my tablets are in my desk drawer. I haven't needed them for months but I'll be as right as rain five minutes after I've taken one."

"No problem. I can't imagine anything worse in this heat."

Nathan pulled up outside the station ten minutes later. "I'll come in, too. I want to ask Amanda to re-schedule one of my appointments."

Amanda was on the phone when he walked in and she gesticulated that he should wait. "Can you just hang on a minute, Mr. Bartholomew? I think I might have heard DCI Costello in another office but I'm not sure. Hold the line while I check will you?" She pressed the mute button. "I've got a Gideon Bartholomew from Kudos Pawnbrokers on the line. Said it was in connection with your recent visit. Do you want to speak to him?"

"I do. I'll take it there. And see if you can put my half-past three appointment back to four, will you?" Nathan stuck up his thumb. "Mr. Bartholomew? DCI Costello speaking. No, no problem. How can I help?"

"You asked me to call you if I remembered anything more about the customer with the 18 carat gold and diamond rings and watch," said Gideon. "Patrick Jones."

"Yes. Have you remembered something?"

"Well, *I* haven't," said Gideon, "but my colleague has. She's got an excellent memory—far better than mine—particularly for trivial things that you or I might not even give a second thought to. It was her day off when you called in the other day, otherwise she would have told you then. Anyway, I was telling her that you'd been making enquiries and we got talking about the rings—they really were beautiful—and that's when she mentioned the young boy."

"Young boy?"

"Yes. He was waiting outside the shop—kept peering through the door and pulling faces at her. I'd forgotten about him until she mentioned it. We wondered if he was the guy's grandson. He gave him some money from the cash we'd just given him and then he rode off on his bike. The kid, that is, not the old guy."

"How old was the boy?"

"Oh, now you're asking." Gideon tutted. "I'm not very good with ages, and Marta's not here just now, but I suppose he was in his teens. Thirteen, fourteen, fifteen, I'm not sure. He had a school uniform on, though; blue blazer with a yellow logo on the pocket. And he had a pack of doughnuts he was munching his way through."

"Doughnuts? Really? Well, that's very interesting. Do you remember what the man did after that?"

"He just walked off, I think. Anyway, I don't know if any of that helps, but I wanted to let you know."

"Yes, it does. It helps very much. Thank you for the call."

"Everything okay?" asked Fiona, looking decidedly sparkier.

"I don't suppose you know what the uniform for St. Eves' secondary school is, do you?"

"Not sure. Do you know, Amanda?"

"Yes, it's a black skirt or trousers, a royal blue blazer and a blue and yellow striped tie." Amanda tapped on her laptop keyboard and beckoned Nathan with her index finger. "See."

Nathan looked at the image of a young boy and girl, both wearing a royal blue blazer with a yellow heraldic shield stitched to the breast pocket. He sighed heavily. "You know, if people just told the truth, everything would be so much easier."

"Why, what's up?"

"After telling us he didn't even *recognise* the name, it's looking very likely that Paul Anderson was actually *with* Patrick Jones the day he left Sunny Days. I'm very close to losing my patience with that young man. Come on, Fiona. The Hula-Hula bar awaits."

ooooooo

On the stone bench, pitted by years of sea salt blasting, Paul Anderson squirmed and shuffled under the scrutiny of the two detectives.

"Why do you want to speak to me about Gavin again? I've already told you everything I know."

"Ah, well, you see, we don't think you have," said Nathan. "And it's not Gavin we want to speak to you about. It's Patrick Jones. We think you know something that you're not telling us. And withholding evidence is a serious offence, you know. Isn't it, DS Farrell?"

"Withholding evidence in a murder investigation? Oh yes, could be very serious," said Fiona. "Very serious indeed."

Paul swallowed, the colour rising up above his shirt collar. "I don't know what you mean," he said, his eyes focused on the floor.

"Could you look at me, please?"

"Huh?"

"I said, could you look at me, please?" repeated Nathan. "I hate talking to the top of someone's head."

Paul raised his gaze and began to chew on a thumbnail.

"Thank you," said Nathan. "Right, can you tell me when you last saw Patrick Jones."

Paul stopped chewing. "I dunno. I already told you, I didn't know him. I don't even recognise the name."

"Yes, I know you *said* that but, the thing is, I don't believe you." Nathan threw him an amiable smile and crossed an ankle over his knee.

Paul shrugged and continued chewing his nail. "Believe what you like. He's dead now, so who's going to dispute whether I knew him or not?"

Doughnuts, Diamonds and Dead Men

"Who indeed?" Nathan stared out to sea. "So you don't know anything about a visit he paid to Kudos Pawnbrokers on the afternoon of the day he disappeared?"

Paul stopped chewing again and visibly gulped.

"Were you involved in Patrick Jones's disappearance? Or what happened to him subsequently?" asked Nathan.

Paul said nothing.

"Look," said Fiona. "You're not in trouble, Paul. Not yet. But if you don't tell us the truth, you could be. If you're withholding anything that may help us solve this case, you could find yourself in a whole lot of trouble."

Paul clasped his hands on top of his head. "For God's sake! It was four years ago! I was only fifteen. And I didn't do anything wrong, I just used to hang around with him sometimes because he was so good to Jemima. And I liked him. I thought he was a good guy—that's not a crime, is it?"

"No, it's not, so why didn't you tell us about it before? Why didn't you tell us that you knew him?"

Paul started on his little finger, spitting the nail out of the side of his mouth. "Because I thought I'd be in trouble if I did. When I saw you in Dad's office the other day, I thought I was *already* in trouble. I thought you'd come for *me*."

Nathan looked at him, his expression quizzical. "Why would we have come for you?"

"Because of the money," said Paul, after a long pause.

"What money?"

"The money I took... I stole."

Nathan looked at Fiona. "What money?"

Paul sighed and stopped chewing.

ooooooo

"So, Patrick pawned one of his rings and his watch for money to give to Jemima to leave Gavin?"

Paul nodded. "Well, for money to give to me to give to Jem. He didn't think she'd take the money if he gave it to her."

"How did you get involved?" asked Fiona. "It was a bit of a gamble for Patrick to give a fifteen-year old boy all that money—I've got a teenage godson and there's no way I'd trust him to give 50p to someone, let alone thousands of pounds. No offence."

Paul half-grinned. "S'okay, none taken. Patrick knew I couldn't stand Gavin and I knew he felt the same. We talked about it all the time. He was a nice old bloke, you know. I was sorry when he went. Anyway, the day he left, he called me to tell me he wanted to meet me from school, which was kind of weird, but he said he needed to talk to me about something urgently.

"He said he was moving on but he couldn't go until he knew that Jemima was going to be okay—he was always telling her to leave Gavin and she was always telling him she didn't have the money to find somewhere else to live. He had this ring—a big, gold signet ring with a massive diamond in it—and this really expensive watch. He told me he was going to sell them and he wanted me to give the money to Jem. Told me to wait until the next day when he'd gone, and then give it to her and tell her to use it to get away from Gavin.

"I asked him why he was going and he just said it was time for him to leave. He said there was no way he wanted to pop his clogs while he was at Sunny Days. He wouldn't tell me where he was going—said it was better that way because if I knew where he was, I might tell Jem and then she'd try to give the money back.

"Anyway, I went with him to the pawn shop and waited outside. He gave me £20 for helping him and told me to go to his room later and he'd give me the money for Jem." He paused and shook his head. "I'd never seen that much money. I meant to give it to her, I really did, but I just couldn't bring myself to, and the longer I left it, the harder it got to even tell her about it, let alone give it to her."

"So you kept it?" asked Fiona.

Paul nodded. "Yeah. I kept it. I even took it to college with me—I couldn't leave it here." He bowed his head. "I didn't spend any of it, though. I tried but I felt so guilty, I couldn't."

"You've still got it?"

"Yeah. Every penny. Am I in trouble?"

"Well, you haven't been very honest but, no, you're not in trouble," said Nathan. "Not with us, anyway. You might be with your sister, though, once you tell her what you've been keeping from her for all these years. Now you've told *us* what happened, you might like to think about telling *her.* If Patrick wanted you to give the money to Jemima, perhaps that's what you should do."

"After keeping it for all this time?" Paul chanced a wry smile. "She'll kick my backside."

"She will if she's got any sense," said Fiona.

"Is that it now? Have you finished with me?"

"Yes, that's it. We knew you'd seen Patrick on the day he disappeared, and we knew you were keeping that from us—we just had to find out why. Go on, get off to your birthday party."

ooooooo

The hubbub in the incident room fell from a rolling boil to a gentle simmer."

"So, we don't know why Patrick Jones left Sunny days, where he was intending to go or what happened to him subsequently.

"Also, we had confirmation this morning that the handwriting on the note which was found next to Gavin Campbell's body is not a match to any of the employees at the garden centre, or any other person of interest who's supplied us with a sample so far. That doesn't mean that our suspects are in the clear, of course, it just means that they didn't write the note.

"Anyway, that's where we are as of now. We're making progress but we're still a long way off solving either of these cases. Any questions? Yes, Carl."

"I don't understand why Patrick Jones would give over fifty grand to Jemima Campbell. I mean, it's not as though she was related or anything. Why would he have done that?"

"Call it a running away fund. He thought Gavin Campbell was an idiot and he wanted to help Jemima get away from him. We've heard from numerous sources how fond he was of her."

"You're not kidding, Chief. He must have been *really* fond of her to have given her over fifty grand. Are we absolutely *sure* there was nothing going on between them? If you get my meaning." Carl winked and encouraged the ensuing cat calls.

"Yes, I think I've got it, loud and clear, thank you, Carl. And if we could curb the suggestive whoops, please; this isn't a playground and we're not fourteen years old. Anyway, to answer your question. No, we're not absolutely sure, but we're as sure as we can be. If anything comes up that points us in another direction, we'll look at it at the time.

"Are we still waiting for the results of Gavin Campbell's phone log, Chief?"

"Yes, but I hope we're going to get something on that later today, or tomorrow. Unfortunately, we found out earlier that Tara Frost, a possible person of interest, is on holiday in Benidorm with her parents and not back for seven days so we'll have to wait till then to speak to her. Right, any more questions before we crack on?"

ooooooo

"DCI Costello!"

When Nathan arrived home that evening, Paul Anderson was sitting on the wall opposite the house, waiting for him.

"Hello. I'm surprised to see you again so soon."

"Sorry to stalk you."

"Have you been waiting long?"

"About three hours."

"Why didn't you come in to the station and have someone call me?"

Paul grinned. "Because I wasn't sure until I saw you just now that I was going to go through with it."

"Go through with what?"

"What I've got to tell you."

"You forgot something earlier?"

Paul stood up, then sat down again. "Sort of."

"What's that supposed to mean?"

"I mean I didn't *forget* to tell you something—I just chose not to." Paul picked at a loose thread on his shorts. "But now I've started, I might as well tell you everything. I might as well tell you what made Patrick decide to give Jem the money. What made him finally decide that she had to leave Gavin, once and for all."

Nathan sat down next to him. "Okay, I'm listening."

"My aunt Holly won a slimming prize a few years back."

"Yes, we know."

"Bet you didn't know she's got a gastric band? That she cheated?"

"Well, we had heard."

"Oh. Who told you?"

"Doesn't matter who told us.

"Oh, right. Well, I bet you don't know why she wanted the money?"

"Not specifically, no. Why did she?"

"Because she had a toy boy. She used to spend it all on him."

"Used to? Is she not seeing him any more?"

"Well, not since he dropped dead. That sort of ended the relationship."

"Oh, sorry to hear that. Was that recently?"

"Last Wednesday."

"I see. She must be very upset."

"Yes, I suppose she is." Paul stared at Nathan until the penny dropped.

"Oh my God! You mean it was your aunt Holly who was seeing Gavin?"

"Yes. And Patrick found out. And then he told me. That's why I can't stand her. And why I hated him so much."

"How did Patrick find out?"

"Because he went round to see her one night to take her to task about cheating to win that money. They were arguing on the doorstep when the front door flew open and Gavin was standing there with a towel wrapped around his waist. I shudder to think what Patrick must have interrupted."

"And what happened?"

"Gavin threatened Patrick. He told him that if he ever breathed a word of Holly's surgery to anyone, or that they were seeing each other, he'd make Jemima's life hell. He knew how much that would get to Patrick because he knew how much he thought of her. Patrick wouldn't have wanted anything he did or said to have made things worse for Jem, so he didn't do anything, or tell anyone. He wanted so badly to expose Holly as a cheat, and to tell Jem that Gavin was being unfaithful, but he couldn't bear to think of what might happen to her if he did. So he kept his mouth shut and said nothing."

"Do you know if anyone else knew about the affair? Your Mum or Dad, for example."

Paul shrugged a shoulder. "Well, I know Patrick told his friend, Nora, that he'd been to see my aunt about the prize money but he didn't tell her about Gavin being there. He thought she might be overcome by a wave of moral conscience and tell someone. My dad? Well, I don't know for sure but if you saw the way he looked at Gavin sometimes, I wouldn't be surprised. Me and dad are convinced that the only reason Gavin wanted to marry Jem was because he knew that, one day, Sunny Days will be left to me and her, along with all my mum and dad's money." Paul ran a hand through his already dishevelled hair. "Tell me, what kind of woman has a relationship with her niece's husband? It's disgusting!" He spat the words from his mouth.

"And ever since I found out about that skeleton, I've been wondering if Holly and Gavin were involved in Patrick's death. But, if that *was* the case, who killed Gavin?" He sighed. "Honestly, I've been going over this for so long, I've hardly slept. If it wasn't for the fact that my mum will go nuts if she finds out about the affair, I probably would have told her but, if I did, I think you'd be arresting *her* for murder soon. Holly's. He shrugged. "And that's it. That's everything."

"Okay," said Nathan. "Thanks for letting me know. I appreciate it."

ooooooo

"Oh my goodness, this gets more and more like a soap opera every day!" Charlotte dished up spaghetti bolognaise into two dishes.

"Tell me about it," said Nathan as he threw a small piece of the parmesan cheese he was grating to each of the dogs.

"Have you spoken to Holly yet?"

"We haven't, but I'm going to now."

"I wonder if she was involved in Patrick's *and* Gavin's deaths?" said Charlotte as she wound spaghetti around her fork.

"Gavin's?"

"Yes—a woman scorned, and all that. If his eye roved as much as you think it probably did, Holly could very well have known about his other women all along. I mean, she seemed like a very nice person but how many times have I said that about people over the past few years only to find out that they're cold-blooded killers? Same motive applies to Jemima Campbell—I know it's a bit of a cliché but people have been bumping off their unfaithful spouses for centuries."

"What other theories do you have?" asked Nathan.

"Well, I wondered if Paul killed Gavin. He's suddenly become very keen to share information with you and I wonder if it's to deflect attention away from him onto someone else?"

"No, he's got an alibi for the time of Gavin's death. The only people who don't are Cooper, Ellen and Jemima."

"Hmm," said Charlotte as she twirled spaghetti around her fork. "Well, I've already told you my thoughts on Jemima. I'd say Cooper's got the strongest motive. If he *did* know about the affair, what more reason could a father need to kill his adulterous son-in-law and, if he *didn't* know about the affair, his motive could simply have been that Gavin treated Jemima terribly. Cooper's a prime suspect, if you ask me." Charlotte waved her fork as she deliberated the evidence.

"As far as Ellen Anderson is concerned, you'd think she'd have been driven by the same motives as her husband but, from what I've heard, it sounds like

Gavin could get away with most things in her eyes, so I'm not sure about her."

Nathan chuckled. "You know what, Agatha? You pose some very interesting theories. Now would you pass the cheese, please?"

CHAPTER THIRTEEN

"Well, it's just been confirmed that Tara Frost's phone number does *not* appear on Gavin Campbell's call log but the number for Holly Simms makes frequent appearances," said Nathan. "There are others on there too that we can't identify, which are being followed up, but Holly's number is by far and away the one he called most often, and for the longest times. Sadly, it's on there even more than Jemima's. The last call he made to Holly's number was at ten-fifty three on the night before his body was found, which is just before he was supposed to meet the person we're assuming was responsible for his death.

"Between half-past eleven and quarter-past one the next morning, Holly Simms called his number a total of seventeen times."

"Blimey, no wonder Paul doesn't like his aunt," said Fiona.

"You're not kidding. Come on, we're going to pay her a visit."

ooooooo

"Miss. Simms? We'd like a quick word with you, if we may? Can we come in?"

Holly walked off without a word, leaving the front door open, and Fiona and Nathan to follow.

"We appreciate that your family have had a terrible shock, what with Gavin Campbell's recent

death. Are you feeling up to answering a few
questions?" asked Fiona.

"I suppose so."

"Actually, we'd like to start by asking about
Patrick Jones. We understand you knew him?"

Holly played with a ringlet, twisting it around
her finger. "Patrick Jones?"

"Yes. He paid you a visit not long before he
disappeared, didn't he? Was that the last time you saw
him?"

Holly took a while to answer. "Yes, he did pay
me a visit. And yes, it was the last time I saw him.
And if you know that he came to see me, then you
must know why. He had a damn cheek, coming round
here, lecturing me on morals. I told him to mind his
own business. It's not illegal what I did, you know. It's
not illegal to lose weight with the help of a gastric
band."

"Well, I think it might be if you're claiming to
have lost the weight that won you the prize money
solely by healthy eating," said Fiona. "And it's terribly
misleading to all the members who are trying to lose
as much weight, as quickly as you did, and who
become disillusioned because they can't."

Holly said nothing.

"Miss. Simms. Did anyone else know about Patrick's visit?" said Nathan. "Your sister or her husband?"

She shook her head. "I didn't tell anyone. Ellen would have panicked about word getting out—she wouldn't have wanted anything to ruin Sunny Days' reputation. And I don't really speak to Cooper much, so I wouldn't have told him anyway."

"I see. And, I'm sorry to ask you this, under the circumstances, but can you tell me when you last saw Gavin Campbell."

Holly shrugged. "I don't know. It must have been when I went round for dinner at Sunny Days when Paul got back from college, I suppose. I didn't have much to do with him."

"So you weren't having a relationship with him?"

Holly blustered. "*What?* Of course not! He was my niece's husband."

"Yes, I'm aware of that," said Nathan. "Which is why I'd be grateful if you could explain the frequency with which your number appears on his phone records."

Holly opened her mouth and then burst into tears. "Please, please don't tell anyone."

Fiona slid a box of tissues toward her. "Did either your sister or her husband know about your relationship?"

Holly stared. "Are you mad? Gavin was their daughter's husband. I mean, Ellen and I are close but I think she might have drawn the line at me bedding down with her son-in-law. And, while I think Cooper would probably have thanked me for taking Gavin off Jemima's hands, I don't he would have been thrilled to know we'd been seeing each other." Her lip quivered as she tried to compose herself.

"So, now can you tell us when you really last saw Gavin?"

"It was the day he died. He stopped off at the leisure centre just after lunch and said he'd be round that evening but he never showed up. And then his body was found the next day. I was really looking forward to that garden centre opening but I'll never set foot in it now. Have you any idea what it's been like living just a few yards away from it since Gavin was killed?"

"You know that his van was found parked at the end of this road?"

"I know. I saw it the next morning. I thought he might have fallen asleep inside it so I looked through the window."

"According to Gavin's call log, he made a call to you at just before eleven. Can you tell us what he said?"

"Just that he had someone to see and he wouldn't be long. That was the last time I spoke to him. When he still hadn't turned up after half an hour, I called him, and kept calling him, but he never answered. Look, I'm sorry, would you mind if we did this later? This is the first time I've talked about Gavin and it's terribly upsetting. Would you mind?"

"Okay," said Nathan. "We'll be in touch."

oooooo

The sun had dipped low in the vermillion-streaked sky when a visitor called at the Costello home.

"Good evening, Charlotte, I'm sorry to call so late. Would it be too much of an imposition to speak to Nathan, if he's at home?"

"Course not. He's just back from walking the dogs and he's jumped in the shower. He won't be long. Actually, you're lucky, this is the first time he's been home before eleven for ages. Come in."

In the living room, Molly sat in her pyjamas, reading a bedtime story to Pippin and Panda who were curled up beside her on the couch, hanging on her every word, one ear cocked at all times.

"...so she ate up *all* the porridge. Oh, hello, Rivron."

"It's 'Reverend', Molly." Charlotte ruffled her hair on her way to call Nathan from the bottom of the stairs.

"Don't worry about it one jot." Reverend Daly grinned. "Good evening, Molly. 1 wasn't expecting to see you up and about." He shook her hand and settled himself in an armchair.

"It's the summer holidays so I don't have to go back to school 'til September. Some days, I'm allowed to stay up until ten o'clock." She studied the Reverend closely as he crossed one trousered leg over the other. "Why aren't you wearing your dress?"

"*Molly!*"

The Reverend chuckled. "Ah, don't worry, Charlotte. I don't wear it all the time, you know, Molly, just for work. If I did, it would get in the way when I went out for my evening walk, so I change into something more suitable. Just like you don't wear your pyjamas all the time."

Molly contemplated his answer before deciding it was a satisfactory explanation. She nodded and closed the book she was reading. "I see. That makes sense. Are you waiting for my Daddy?"

"Yes, I am."

"I'm going to bed in a minute. He probably didn't hear when mummy called him because he sings in the shower. I can tell him you're here if you like?"

"That would be splendid, Molly. Thank you."

Two minutes after Charlotte had taken Molly up to bed, closely followed by the dogs who were her constant guardians until morning, Nathan appeared.

"Evening, Reverend. You wanted to talk to me?"

"Hello, Nathan. Yes, I did, if you can spare me a few minutes."

"I can spare you as long as you like. Can I get you anything? Tea, coffee, whisky?"

Reverend Daly rubbed his hands together. "Ah, well, now you're talking. I wouldn't say no to a shot of the golden nectar...as you're offering." Partial to a single malt, the Reverend took the glass Nathan handed him, a glint in his eye as he tipped it to his lips. "There was never a finer drop," he said, as he savoured the taste.

"So, what is it you wanted to talk to me about?" asked Nathan. "It must be important for you to call round at this time of night."

"Well, I was taking my evening constitutional anyway, so I was already out, but something came to me earlier that I thought you should know. I feel like such an eejit for not remembering it before."

"What is it?"

"I don't know what made me think of it but, while I was eating my dinner, I recalled seeing a man kneeling beside a grave one evening, some time ago. Nothing unusual about that, of course, so at the time, I put it from my mind. I was curious enough to wonder whose grave he'd been visiting, though, so the next morning, I took a look." Reverend Daly supped the last of his whisky.

"And whose grave *was* it?"

"It was the Jones family grave."

"When was this?"

"Well, when I remembered about seeing the man, I thought back to when that could be and I remembered that I was in a rush because I was on my way to see a parishioner who was terribly ill and I was running late, which is why I didn't stop and talk to him. Anyway, I checked back in my old diaries before I came out tonight and it turns out it was the day before Patrick disappeared. Time was getting on so I just locked up the church and left."

"Did you recognise him?"

"No, I didn't. I'm sorry I didn't remember this before, Nathan, but it just didn't occur to me until a couple of hours ago."

"Don't worry about it." Nathan stroked his chin. "The grave—has anyone been to visit it since Patrick left, do you know?"

"Not to my knowledge. As you know, there are gardeners who tend the cemetery. They keep the area surrounding the graves as free from weeds and long grass as they can, but the upkeep of the graves themselves are the responsibility of the family, and I don't believe that Henry and Flo had any family other than Patrick and Lucy, did they?"

"Well, there was an aunt and uncle who passed away some years before Patrick left St. Eves, and a cousin, but he lives in Canada so it's unlikely to have been him you saw."

Reverend Daly put his empty glass on the coffee table. "Well, I'd better be going, I suppose." He glanced at his watch. "Oh, is that all it is? I thought it was much later."

Nathan didn't miss the twinkle in his eye. "Another single malt, Reverend?"

"Ah, well, seeing as you're offering," Reverend Daly proffered his glass, "it'd be rude not to!"

oooooo

The following day, Nathan changed the usual route for his early-morning run to go past All Saints church.

There were two routes to the top of the hill on which All Saints stood. One was via the old, stone staircase which had been cut into the hillside and the other was via the road which meandered up from the town. Opting for the stairs, the muscles in Nathan's legs were burning by the time he reached the top.

He stretched and took a long draught from his water bottle. He'd omitted to ask Reverend Daly where the Jones family grave was, so he started at the headstones closest to the church and searched up and down the rows in a methodical fashion.

Ten minutes later, he found what he was looking for; an unkempt plot, overgrown with scorched grass, and daisies pushing their way towards the sunlight through white marble gravel. The gold-lettered inscription on the headstone read, "Let no hand touch the stones that keep, Flo, Henry and Lucy in heavenly sleep."

He stared at the grave for a while before jogging away, pondering the identity of its mystery visitor.

oooooo

"Okay. You'll let us know if you find a match for the print? Great. Thanks."

Gathering his belongings in preparation for a meeting, Nathan looked up at the knock on his door.

"Ah, hello Carl. I was about to call at the incident room on my way out. I've just had forensics on the line about the box that SOCO found at the garden centre near Gavin Campbell's body."

"Oh, right. What did they have to say about it?"

"Well, they weren't wasp droppings."

"What were they, then?"

"Hornet droppings. And, before you ask, they're one of the few stinging insects that *do* come out at night. They're attracted to light, apparently."

"And what about the fingerprint in the paté? Did they have any luck with that?"

"Not yet but they'll get back to us if they find a match. Anyway, what can I do for you?"

"Have you got a minute, Chief?"

"Well, I'm on my way out but you can walk with me if you like. What's up?"

Carl scratched his head. "This investigation is throwing up surprise after surprise." He flapped a piece of paper in the air.

"Such as?"

"Well, I've been calling that number you gave me. The one for John Jones in Canada. Because of the time difference, I've been trying at different times during the day to get to speak to someone and it wasn't until the thirteenth time of trying that I eventually got hold of someone half an hour ago."

"Oh, good. Lucky for some. And is it still his number?"

"Well, yes. And no."

Nathan gave him a sideways look. "I haven't got time for riddles, Carl."

"Well, it's the number of his home in Canada, but he's not there. Hasn't been there for four years."

"Where is he, then?"

"He's here, Chief."

Nathan stopped walking. "What do you mean, "he's here"?"

"I spoke to his housekeeper and she told me that Mr. Jones has been staying with his cousin Patrick since he went to visit four years ago. At an address in St. Matlock. Wanted to get back in touch with his English roots, she said. He was born here, see. Dual-nationality."

"So, let me get this straight. John Jones came to St. Eves to visit Patrick four years ago?"

"That's what the lady said."

"And he's been staying a few miles down the road ever since?"

"Apparently. The housekeeper said she still speaks to him fairly regularly."

"Did this housekeeper give you any contact details for him?"

Carl showed him a slip of paper. "An address and a mobile number, Chief."

"Well, I'll be…" Nathan turned and started walking back the way he'd just come. "Excellent work, Carl. I'll arrange for Ben and Fiona to get over to that address. Amanda, cancel my appointments for the rest of the day, will you." Nathan took off his jacket and unfastened his top button. "I've got a feeling we might finally be on to something in the search for Patrick Jones's killer. If anyone wants me, I'll be in the incident room."

ooooooo

"Chief, that address for John Jones is just a postal address—there's no one living here." Fiona updated Nathan on developments from the address John Jones's housekeeper had given Carl.

"It's a building with a whole load of post boxes that are used by a number of people. There's a sign on the door with a number to call if you want to hire a box so we've managed to track down the woman who rents them out." "She doesn't know anyone by name—she meets with them when they register their name for a box and, after that, she remembers them by their post box number. Our guy is Mr. twenty-six. She said he was "just an ordinary old guy." Her words not mine. And she recalls that he was casually dressed, with a beard, grey hair, and he wore a baseball cap and mirrored sunglasses. She remembered him because she's tall—six foot—and he was taller than her by at least an inch."

"She must be able to give us a name, for heaven's sake?"

"Yes, Ben's waiting for a call back from her. She just couldn't remember what it was off the top of her head—there are over fifty post boxes here, you see. She's just checking her files. I thought I'd give you a quick update while we were waiting. Oh, hang on, I think this is her calling Ben now."

Ben swiped a finger across his phone. "Hi. Yes. Right. And that's definite, is it? Okay, thanks for your help."

"Well? Has she got a name for Mr. twenty-six?"

"Yes. It's John Jones."

oooooo

"Chief, I've got Wendy Myers on the line."

"Good, I've been waiting to speak to her. Hi, Wendy—you wouldn't believe what's going on down here. Anyway, I hope you've got good news."

"Well, I've got good news," she paused, "and not so good news. Which do you want first?"

"Give me the good news—it'll bolster me up for the bad."

"Well, the good news is that I can tell you what type of object those head injuries were caused by."

"That *is* good news. What was it?"

"The first, smaller head wound was made by a blunt, pointed object with a width of three centimetres and a depth of two centimetres. The second, larger wound was also made by a blunt object, but this was round in shape, similar to a golf ball, but bigger at five centimetres in diameter. This object was also responsible for all the other wounds present. As I said before, all the injuries look to have been made with considerable force."

"Okay, what's the not so good news?"

"Well, it's odd. Those items you bought in that belonged to Patrick Jones; the book and the scarf in particular."

"Yes, what about them?"

"Well, we've got some great DNA samples from them—from skin cells and hair."

"What's odd about that? That's good, isn't it?"

"Well, normally, yes. But in this case, none of them match the DNA we took from the skeleton."

CHAPTER FOURTEEN

Having just called Nathan so that Molly could say hello, Charlotte had learned from a very brief conversation that some progress had been made in the investigation into Patrick Jones's murder; forensics had established what type of weapon had been used to kill him. She'd made the call short. She could hear from the chatter around him that he was busy.

Ever since the trip to Sutton's Folly, she'd tried to forget about Patrick Jones. However, the more she tried to forget, the more thoughts of him, his family, and the letters he'd written to Betty, pervaded her mind.

The circumstances surrounding Patrick's life before St. Eves, his tragic family history, his disappearance and the subsequent discovery of his remains, had bothered her for days.

Something about the whole business was nagging at her. Like there was something she was desperately trying to remember, but just couldn't quite recall. She knew it was there, it the back of her mind but, for the life of her, she couldn't bring it to the fore.

She was planning on having a chat with Ava to see if she had any thoughts which might put a new perspective on the situation, and an afternoon at the beach was the perfect opportunity.

"Are you ready, Molly? When the shuttlecock comes to you, try to hit it to Ava this time, okay?"

Charlotte hit the shuttlecock and Molly caught it square on her racquet.

"That's it, dear. Well done! Now pass it over here to me, and I'll... Ooh, I say!" Ava dodged the shuttlecock as it whistled past her nose, catapulted through the air by Molly's overarm smash.

"Ava! You're supposed to hit it to Mummy!"

"Sorry, dear. I was distracted. This blasted headband keeps slipping over my eyes." Ava pulled up her sweatband and tapped her racquet against the palm of her hand. "Actually, isn't it time for lunch?" She glanced at her watch. "My stomach's rumbling."

"You know, you'll never learn how to play if you keep making excuses," said Molly. She slipped her hand into Ava's and grinned up at her. "It's okay, we'll play something different after lunch. Which one do you like best out of all these? Frisbee, handstands, cartwheels, catch, rounders or bat and ball?"

"Well, to be honest, dear, beach games have never really been my thing." Ava squeezed her hand. "But I can teach you how to salsa dance after lunch if you like?"

Molly's eye's widened and she thrust her hand under Ava's nose. "Deal!"

oooooooo

Picnic lunch over, Molly dozed in the shade of a vast sun umbrella, Pippin and Panda curled up beside her.

"Ava, did you know Patrick Jones's parents?" Charlotte's tone was casual as she packed up the wicker basket.

"His parents? No, dear. I knew *of* them but I didn't actually *know* them, per se. Why do you ask?"

"Because I'm trying to find out a bit more about Patrick's background—you know, in the hope that it might give some clues as to what happened to him."

"But the police are already investigating, dear. Don't you think you should leave well alone?"

"I know they are, Ava, but with Gavin Campbell passing away recently, it seems that most of their focus has been on him, and I know that Betty's dying to know what happened to Patrick. Every time I see her, she asks if Nathan's had any luck with finding out, so I thought I'd have a sniff around myself to see if I can dig up anything new."

"Does Nathan know what you're up to?"

Charlotte side-stepped the question. "Wouldn't you feel happier knowing that Patrick's killer was behind bars? I know I would. Anything I can find out has got to be a good thing, don't you think?"

Ava's face took on a pained expression. "The thing is, dear, every time you take matters into your own hands, you always seem to end up in trouble. I seem to recall the last time you took it upon yourself to do a little sleuthing on the side, you ended up locked in a store room tied to a chair."

Charlotte waved a dismissive hand. "Oh, that's all in the past. I'm not going to get into anything risky, I'm just trying to find out some things."

"Well, as long as you're not going to put yourself in any danger." Ava applied a slick of sunblock to her nose and settled back in her deckchair.

"What about his parents' friends." Charlotte persisted. "Any ideas who they were?"

"Not a clue, I'm afraid. Contrary to popular belief, I don't know *everything* about *everyone* in St. Eves, you know. Whoever they were, though, I doubt if many of them are still around. I'm sure Betty said that Patrick's parents passed away a year or so before he turned up at Sunny Days, so they must have been a good age. That being the case, if their friends were of similar ages, I should think they've all kicked the bucket by now."

She pulled her sunhat over her face. "Why don't you ask Reverend Daly? He's been at All Saints for years—he must have known them, even if only casually. At the very least, he would have officiated at their funerals, so he will have had some dealings with the family then, even if at no other time."

Charlotte pointed at Ava with the cucumber she was holding. "Of course! That's brilliant! Why didn't I think of that? Ava, you're a gem. Yes, I'll pop round to the church later."

"Promise you won't get too involved in this, dear?" Ava lifted her hat. "You don't want to go getting into trouble like you have in the past."

"I promise. I've just got this feeling about this case. Don't ask me what it is, because I don't know—I just know that something doesn't feel right and, when I get a feeling like that, it's like an itch that needs scratching. You know what I mean? It's like I know something isn't right but I've no idea what. I didn't even know Patrick, or his family, but I can't shake this feeling that something doesn't quite fit. It's weird, don't you think? Ava?"

The brim of Ava's sunhat over her face fluttered in the breeze of her gentle snores. Four minutes of beach badminton had taken its toll.

Charlotte grinned and settled back in her chair. She was keen to speak to Reverend Daly, but the visit would keep until after a lazy afternoon in the sun.

oooooooo

"Mummy, I need my new pink pyjamas for the sleepover. The ones with the yellow flowers on them. Did you remember to pack them?"

Charlotte laughed at her daughter who was ticking things off a long list with a concerned expression on her face. "Yes, little miss bossy boots, I've packed them. And your pink slipper socks with the puppies on the front."

Molly's frown disappeared. "Yay! Thank you, Mummy. You know, it's a shame Pippin and Panda can't come with me. They'd love sleeping out in the tent." She gave Charlotte a sideways glance. "D'you think they could come too?"

Charlotte shook her head. "I should think the last thing you need in the tent with three overexcited girls are two overexcited dogs. No, they'll be better off here, sweetheart. In any case, I wouldn't dream of asking Sharon and Charlie to look after our dogs for the night. They're more of a handful than you, you little monkey, and that's saying something." She pulled Molly into a hug. "Right, come on, you, put your shoes on and we'll get going."

ooooooo

Having dropped Molly off for her sleepover with best friends, Esme and Erin Donovan, Charlotte made her way to All Saints, the centuries-old stone church that perched high on the hill, overlooking the bay.

She could hear the congregation belting out 'All Things Bright and Beautiful', so she waited for Reverend Daly on a bench in the church gardens.

The adjoining cemetery was surrounded by lovingly-tended lawns which grew almost to the hill's edge, stopping at the ancient stone wall that circled its perimeter. Now, with the early evening sunlight dappling the old stone of the church through the trees, Charlotte thought she had never seen All Saints look more beautiful.

"The Lord God made them aaaallllll."

The hymn came to an end, shortly followed by the heavy vestibule door being flung open. Reverend Daly appeared, followed by his parishioners as they spilled out of the church into the grounds. He shook every hand and spoke a few words to each one of them before turning and raising his hand in welcome.

"Ah, Charlotte. Are you here for the choir practice? You know we're always on the lookout for new members."

"Me? Oh, no! Oh my gosh, no. You wouldn't want me in the choir—I've got a voice like a cow with its tail caught in a milking machine. No, I wondered if I could have a quick chat with you? It won't take long."

"Well, I'm popping home for a while before the last service but you're welcome to walk with me. Between you and me, I'm gasping for a cuppa. All that singing and sermon-ing in this heat makes you awfully parched, y'know."

"Yes, I can imagine it does." She fell in step beside him. "Um, I wondered if you could tell me anything about Patrick Jones's parents. I know you've been at the church for a long time so I thought you'd probably have known them."

Reverend Daly's pace slowed. "Why d'you ask?"

"Well, I'm trying to find out a bit more about him in the hopes it will shed some light on what happened. I suppose I feel I'd like to do something to help because Betty Tubbs is a good friend of mine and she's been so upset since he was found. They were close friends, you know."

The Reverend's face took on a sombre expression. "Yes, I know they were. I didn't know Patrick very well myself; his parents came to services every Sunday and sometimes during the week, but he wasn't a churchgoer. I used to see him around town, though, and I presided at the funerals of both his parents, so I knew him to pass the time of day with."

"I don't suppose you'd happen to know if any of the people who attended his parents' funerals are still around? It would be good if I could speak to some of them."

Reverend Daly puffed out his cheeks. "To be honest with you, the turnout for the funeral wasn't great. The Jones family were friendly enough but, from the day they moved here, they tended to keep themselves to themselves. And I'm pretty sure that most of the people who *did* come to the funerals are no longer with us. Although… Hmmm, I wonder?" He clasped his hands behind his back as he strode along. "You know, Charlotte, there *is* someone but whether she'll be willing to talk to you is another matter. She knew the family as well as anyone."

"Oh, that's great. Who is she?"

"Annie Bray. She was a neighbour—a few years younger than Patrick's parents. She got quite friendly with Patrick's mother when his father became ill. The strain of caring for him was hard on her and Annie took a lot of the pressure off, so I understand."

"And you think she's still around?"

"Well, I haven't heard anything to the contrary, put it that way. Last I heard of her was last year, when she sent a message via her daughter that she wouldn't be attending the Christmas service because it was too cold for her, and too far to come. They'd not long moved into a place on the St. Matlock Road. Mind you, she'll be well into her nineties now, and if her health's not good she may not be able to help you at all. Could be worth a try, though."

"Okay. Have you got an address?"

"I think it's just Magnolia Cottage. If you take the St. Matlock Road, be on the lookout for a red-brick house with the most beautiful Magnolia tree that God ever put on this earth, in the front garden. You'll need to drive for a good ten minutes before you come to it but you can't miss it. It's at the…now let me see." He counted on his fingers. "The first, second, third, fourth, fifth, yes, the fifth junction you come to and it sticks out like a sore thumb, but in a good way." He looked at his watch. "In fact, I've got a little time, I can call her daughter if you like? She used to ring the church bells so I'll have her number somewhere. It'll only take a minute and it'll be better than you just turning up on the doorstep, not knowing her from Adam."

Charlotte nodded her appreciation. "That'd be great, if you wouldn't mind. If she's okay to see me, I'll take a drive out later if that suits. Thanks, Reverend, you've been very helpful."

oooooooo

In the absence of a bell on the door of the red-brick house, there was a doorknocker which came off in Charlotte's hand as soon as she touched it. She rapped her knuckles against the old wood. A few minutes passed before the door was flung open by a woman with smiling eyes and springy, mahogany curls which refused to be contained by the faded baseball cap pulled over them. She welcomed Charlotte with a grin and a comfortable familiarity.

"You must be Charlotte? Pleased to meet you. I'm Sara."

"I'm sorry about this." Charlotte handed her the doorknocker. "I barely touched it and it came off."

Sara smacked her hand against her forehead, leaving a terracotta handprint behind. "Damn it! I knew there was something I meant to do." She took the doorknocker from Charlotte and beamed an apologetic smile. "Sorry about that—it's been loose for ages. Almost came off in the postman's hand last Thursday and I completely forgot to fix it. Memory like a sieve, you know. And excuse me for not shaking hands, won't you? I've been at the wheel all afternoon and I've got clay in places I didn't even know I had places." She covered her mouth in a child-like way when she giggled, and Charlotte warmed to her immediately.

Chattering all the way, she led Charlotte through the house. "Mum lives in the annexe. She wouldn't want to live in the house with us—she's far too independent—and, to be honest, it would drive us all round the twist if she did. No, on the other side of the wall suits us all very nicely, thank you very much. Close enough to be together when we want to be, but far enough to keep us all sane."

She grinned as she took Charlotte out of the back door to a small courtyard which housed a smart, single-storey, red-brick annexe with a pitched roof and its own front door, complete with stained-glass panel.

"I'll just pop in and tell her you're here. And make sure she's decent. We never know quite what to expect when we visit. My husband took the Sunday papers round last week and found her eating breakfast in one of my swimsuits and a pair of wellington boots. She greeted him as though it was a perfectly normal way to dress for breakfast. And when the doctor called round to see her last month when she had a chest infection, she was wearing one of my grand-daughter's tee-shirts. Mum borrows things from the washing line if they take her fancy, you see, and this particular shirt had a slogan on the front that said, 'Wake Me Up When it's Time to Get Down'."

Charlotte giggled.

"Yes, I thought it was funny, too," said Sara, "until the doctor made the mistake of talking about Mum as though she wasn't in the room. He asked me how long she'd been experiencing signs of unusual age-related behaviour. Anyway, she hit him over the head with her backscratcher and told him in no uncertain terms that she's not doolally, just eccentric." She snorted at the recollection before disappearing through the door, returning a few minutes later.

"You can go in but I warn you, she's just woken up from a nap so she might be a little cranky."

"Oh, don't worry about that, I can handle cranky."

"And mind you don't sit on a cat. They blend in with the furniture after a while."

Charlotte grinned and pushed open the door, stepping into a room filled with an abundance of light, antique furniture and cats.

She approached a high-backed chair facing the window, on the narrow arms of which sat two fat tabbies who eyed her with suspicion as she drew near. One of them let out a loud meow and a hiss, its back suddenly arching as it stood perfectly still and focused on her, as if about to launch into a routine on a balance beam.

"Sit down, Churchill, don't be so hostile," Annie Bray scolded, and the cat turned a perfect circle on its narrow apparatus before settling down again.

"Well? Come round here, girl, where I can see you," barked the elderly woman, jabbing at the air with her long, wooden backscratcher.

Charlotte gave it a wide berth and made her way around to the front of the chair where Annie regarded her through inquisitive eyes of the brightest cerulean, the perfect foil for her snow-white hair and rosy complexion.

"You the girl who wants to talk to me about Flo and Henry Jones?"

"Yes, if you don't mind. I won't disturb you for too long."

"Hmpf, you'd better not. I've got lots to do this evening and I don't have time to sit around gossiping." Annie banged on a chair opposite her with her walking stick. "Well, sit down, sit down."

For a woman in her nineties, Annie didn't look anywhere near ready to be hanging up her stick any time soon.

"So, what d'you want to know?"

"Well, you probably know about the remains that were found recently, just off the coast."

"Patrick's, you mean? Course I do. I read the papers every day. Why?"

"Well, it must have been quite a shock. Did you know him very well?"

Annie wrapped her arthritic fingers around her backscratcher and stroked one of the cats between the ears while he adopted a regal pose at her side, his purr resonating around the room. "I wouldn't say I knew him *very* well but I knew him well enough. He was like a square peg in a round hole, that one. Never really got used to living in a town. Proper country boy, he was.

"I remember when one of the cats got bitten by an adder one summer. Patrick knew it wasn't a grass snake because there were only two puncture wounds— grass snakes have got more teeth, apparently, so they make more holes in the flesh when they bite. Anyway, that's the sort of thing he knew about and he knew I had to get Chalky to the vet as soon as possible. If it had been left to me, I would have just washed it and put antiseptic on it but Patrick knew otherwise. It's the only time I've ever been grateful to him for popping round unannounced. If it hadn't been for him, Chalky wouldn't have lasted the day, most likely, but he went on for another ten years.

"I knew his parents better than I knew him. I helped his mother when she was caring for his father during his illness, and then I helped care for her when she became ill herself, but I didn't have a lot to do with Patrick. Not if I could help it, anyway. He'd call round here every now and then, especially after his parents died—always uninvited and always for a good old moan. I think he used to visit because I was the only person left who'd known his mum and dad well, but apart from that, I had nothing to do with him." She gazed out of the window. "Between you and me, I thought he was a bit of a pillock."

"Did you? Why was that, then?"

"You're a nosy one, aren't you?" Annie gave Charlotte a sly smile. "Oh, don't look so put out, I don't mind. I like a good gossip. Makes a nice change from talking about my bowel movements—Sara likes to keep track, you see."

She pointed to a pile of photograph albums with her walking stick. "Bring those over here, will you? Yes, those. And put them down here—that's right." She took a sip from a carton of apple juice beside her. "The reason I didn't have a lot of time for Patrick was because, to put it mildly, he was an irresponsible, good-for-nothing, lazy layabout who couldn't be trusted. And he was a spoiled brat. Didn't like it if he couldn't get his own way. He did have one redeeming characteristic, mind you—he couldn't tolerate any kind of abuse towards women—but, apart from that, he was an idiot."

Considering her scathing review, it occurred to Charlotte that, perhaps, Annie was confused as to who Patrick was and was referring to someone else. "Erm, you *are* talking about Patrick Jones, aren't you? Flo and Henry Jones's son?"

Annie glared and banged her walking stick on the floor. "Of *course* I am, girl!" she roared. "I already said that, didn't I? Who else would I be talking about?"

"Oh. Right. Okay." Charlotte held up a placatory hand. "It's just that I've spoken to quite a few people about him and you're the first person who's mentioned that. Almost everyone else has been very complimentary."

"Well, I expect that's because other people didn't know him like I did. I bet they don't know that he frittered away the inheritance his parents left him and when there was no more, he begged his cousin for more? And that when *that* was gone, he wanted even more but his cousin refused to give it to him?"

Charlotte was convinced now that Annie was confused. She was getting the cousins mixed up.

"You mean, the cousin in Canada asked *Patrick* for money, don't you?"

"Are. You. Being. Deliberately. Dense?" Annie spoke slowly. "No, I mean that Patrick asked his cousin, John, for more money when his inheritance was running low and he bailed him out once but told him there wouldn't be a second time. Are you with me, girl?"

Charlotte frowned. "I'm sorry, no. I'm really confused."

"Well, it's quite simple—I don't know why you can't grasp it." Annie took another sip of her apple juice and smacked her lips together.

"Well…I don't understand why Patrick was asking John for money. I mean, why would he? You know, seeing as he'd already inherited a fortune."

Annie spluttered. ""Inherited a fortune"? Where on earth did you hear that? *Patrick* didn't inherit a fortune, *John* did. It was *John's* parents who had all the wealth—not Patrick's. Not that Henry and Flo didn't leave Patrick a nice little nest egg after they died, but he went to Canada to visit John and spent most of it while he was there. He asked John if he'd give him some more money, which he did, but he told him that was the last of the lump sum payments. He said he'd be happy to give him a monthly allowance, if he was struggling, but Patrick told him to stick it.

"He came to see me when he got home from the visit and I still remember how furious he was that John had so much wealth while he had so little. He couldn't bear that people might view him as the poor relation. Mind you, he said he'd left Canada with a nice little insurance policy that would top up his pension nicely—don't ask me what he meant because I have no idea. All I know is that he thought he was as entitled to his aunt and uncle's fortune as John was.

"I know he used to like to pretend he had more money than he knew what to do with but, truth is, until his parents died he barely had two pennies to rub together and they weren't particularly well off, anyway. His aunt and uncle, on the other hand, had a successful business which they handed over to John when they retired and, so Flo told me, John's mother's side of the family were super-rich. They had diamonds and a huge personal fortune which was all left to John when his parents passed away."

Charlotte was listening so intently, she barely moved when one of the tabbies jumped onto the chair beside her and began to open and close its paws on her thigh.

"I can tell by the look on your face that you've been told a different story?" said Annie.

Charlotte nodded. "*Totally* the opposite. As I understand, Patrick used to say that *John* was the jealous one because the family fortune *hadn't* been left to him. According to Patrick, *John* had always been the irresponsible one, and careless with his finances, so both sets of parents had decided that the money and assets would be safer with Patrick. He told everyone it was *his* side of the family that had diamonds and wealth, not John's."

Annie chuckled. "That doesn't surprise me at all. Patrick lived in a fantasy world most of the time. Always trying to impress people and pretending he was something he wasn't." Annie took a photograph album from the top of the pile and began to flick through the pages.

"Was that the last time you saw him?" Charlotte asked. "When he came to see you after he got back from Canada?"

Annie shook her head. "No, the last time I saw him was when he came to tell me that John had been in touch, completely out of the blue. He'd told him he was coming to St. Eves and that he had something for him."

"What was it, do you know?"

Annie shrugged a shoulder. "No idea. I never saw him again."

"And how long ago was that?"

"It was a few days before he left the retirement home."

Charlotte's mind was racing. What Annie had told her went against everything she knew about Patrick. *Why had he lied about being wealthy? And did his cousin's visit to St. Eves have anything to do with his death?*

Ah, here they are." Annie handed her the photograph album. "Thought you might be interested in seeing some photos of Flo and Henry. There's a few of them in the garden at their house in Wyndham Street. Oh, and some more that were taken at a street party we had for St. George's Day. They didn't socialise much but that was one of the few occasions they did.

"They were a troubled family, you know. Something terrible happened before they came to live in St. Eves but I have no idea what. All I know is that they used to live in a place called Folly, something or other, but, whenever I asked her why they left, Flo would get terribly upset and couldn't talk about it."

"Really?" Charlotte looked up from the photograph album but didn't offer any information on what she knew about Patrick's sister.

Annie reached over with her walking stick and tapped it on the book. "That's the street party. That's Flo in the green dress at the front and that's Henry and Patrick behind her."

As Charlotte glanced down at the photos, she saw something that made the hairs stand up on the back of her neck. And the longer she stared at it, the more she knew she'd found the memory which had been so elusive. She tried to keep the excitement from her voice.

"Annie, would you mind if I borrowed this photo, please? I'll take good care of it and I'll bring it back when I've finished with it. I'm sure I won't be needing it for long."

Annie looked pleased to have been of service. "Yes, of course, if you like. What's so special about it?"

"I think it'll help to prove what killed Patrick Jones."

She bid Annie goodbye and thanked her for her help before joining the evening rush-hour traffic. She had Nathan on auto dial but her calls repeatedly went through to his answerphone.

She glanced across at the photograph on the dashboard.

The photograph which showed what she was certain was the murder weapon which had been used to inflict such terrible injuries on Patrick Jones.

She remembered all the things Nathan had told her about the weapon they were hoping to identify. A blunt, pointed object... Similar to a golf ball, but bigger...

And she remembered the day Patrick had come into the café with Betty. The day he'd cut his foot and left his walking stick behind. The walking stick with the heavy brass handle, fashioned from a large round dog's head with close-set ears and a blunt, pointed muzzle.

Someone had murdered Patrick with his own walking stick.

ooooooo

"I've got Nora Tweedie on the line, Chief. Says it's urgent. She thinks Betty Tubbs is in trouble."

"In trouble? Hello, Nora. Yes, this is DCI Costello. No, don't worry. Pardon? I see. Yes. Uh-huh. Her curtains are closed? Yes. *What*?! Oh, my God. Alright, yes, we'll be there right away."

Nathan grabbed his keys. "We need to get to Betty's asap. I'll explain on the way. You're not going to believe what Nora Tweedie's just told me."

CHAPTER FIFTEEN

Each retirement bungalow sat on its own neat plot of land, the lawns cut and the rose bushes lovingly tended by a team of diligent gardeners.

In her spotless kitchen, and revived by a long nap after kneading dough for her bread machine, Betty hummed tunelessly as she tipped a ladle, sending a steaming river of tomato and basil soup into her bowl. She sprinkled a handful of chopped chives on top and laid it on the table beside a plate containing a cheese sandwich, and a small glass of white wine.

Switching on the TV, she was about to start dinner when the doorbell rang.

"Oh bother. Why do people always call when you least want them to?" She sighed and made her way to the door, the dark shadow on the other side of the frosted glass giving no clue to the identity of her caller.

"Yes?" She smiled at the man. "Actually, I'm just about to have my dinner so if you could call back in half an hour, that would suit me better. Are you selling something?"

"No." The man's gruff voice was muffled behind the collar of his jacket which was zipped up past his bearded chin, and the peak of his cap cast a shadow over his face and his mirrored sunglasses.

It occurred to Betty that, considering the warmth of the evening, a jacket was totally unnecessary, let alone one that was fastened all the way to the top.

"Well, as I was saying, I was just about to eat so if you could... Just a minute, I recognise you. You're the man from the garden centre, aren't you? You bumped into me? What do you want? I hope you're not following me. I'm very good friends with the DCI, you know, so..."

She was still talking when her visitor stepped into the house, pushed her backwards and slammed the front door behind him.

ooooooo

He spoke in a heavily accented voice. "Now, don't panic. I don't want to hurt you. If you just sit down and be quiet, I'll take what I came for and leave before anyone even knows I was here. But, please, don't make any noise."

He lowered Betty onto the couch before striding to the living room window and closing the curtains, shutting out the early evening sunlight. As the room dimmed, Betty opened her mouth to protest, closing it when he put his finger to his lips.

His eyes searched the room, his breath quickening as they fell upon the painting Patrick had given Betty. He reached above the fireplace to remove it from the wall, putting it into a bag he produced from his pocket.

Betty's eyes followed him. *What on earth does he want with that old thing?*

There was something about the man that unsettled her. Tall and straight-backed, he reminded her of someone, but his features were almost completely obscured by his beard, sunglasses and hat.

"It's not worth anything, you know." Betty hoped that if she could persuade him she had nothing worth stealing, he would leave her alone

He chuckled. "Not to you, maybe."

The sudden sound of nearby chattering outside startled him. He raised a warning hand to stop Betty from calling out and peered through a chink in the curtains to see a group of senior citizens congregating on the wooden benches on the pavement.

"That'll be the bingo crowd," said Betty. "It doesn't start 'til eight but they always meet up far too early and then spend half-an-hour nattering while they wait for everyone to arrive." Her shoulders sagged and she cast her eyes downwards when she heard a high-pitched laugh. "That's Nora Tweedie. We used to go to bingo together but we, er, we had a difference of opinion and... Anyway, I don't go any more."

She looked up at the man. "Sorry, I'm supposed to be being quiet, aren't I?" She gave him a nervous smile. "By the way, if you're waiting to leave without being seen, I doubt that lot," she jerked her thumb towards the window, "will be going anywhere for a while. You might as well sit down and make yourself comfortable—all that pacing about is making me nervous."

The man stared for a long while before perching on the edge of the armchair furthest away from Betty.

They sat, without speaking, until a loud bell broke the silence.

The man jumped up, turning quickly and tripping over the edge of the rug as he stepped back. He fell awkwardly, losing his toupee, his cap, and a shoe as it skidded across the floor.

"It's alright, it's just the timer on the bread machine." Betty watched the man as he scrabbled to reach the hairpiece and the cap, quickly pulling the former over his bald head and the latter back down over his face as he heaved himself to his feet.

His shoe had come to a stop some distance away and Betty could see that something from inside it had fallen out. The man moved swiftly to retrieve it and the breath caught in her throat. He only took two steps but they were enough for her to see that, without his shoe, his foot fell noticeably short of the floor, causing him to walk with a limp. She tried to swallow and found her mouth devoid of saliva.

"It can't be." Her eyes darted to the man's face to find his eyes avoiding her.

He picked up the shoe and replaced the wedge-shaped object which had become dislodged. He slipped his foot into it and the limp vanished.

"Patrick?" Betty's voice was barely a breath. "It can't be," she repeated. "Is it you?" She moved towards him, her outstretched hand coming to rest on his arm. "It is you, isn't it? I should have known—you're still talking in those silly voices after all these years. And why are you wearing a wig? And a lift in your shoe?"

The man's jaw clenched before he slumped down and slung the cap and the toupee across the couch. "How else do you think I'd have managed to come and go without being noticed?"

"Oh my Lord, I don't believe it!" Betty's knees gave way and she dropped onto the couch beside him. "We thought you were dead! Where have you been? And what are you doing here?" She smacked him on the arm. "And why didn't you tell me it was you when I saw you at the garden centre?"

Patrick sighed. "It's a long story, and I'll get to all of it in time. It was a risky thing to do, but I'd been walking around St. Eves for days without anyone knowing it was me. I knew that if anyone would see through the disguise, it would be you or Nora. I had to know if you recognised me. Especially as I knew I'd be paying you a visit."

"Oh my goodness. I can't take this in. Pass me that glass of wine on the table, will you?" Betty took the glass and downed it in one. She eyed him warily. "Do you know that a skeleton was found a few weeks ago? And that everyone thought it was yours because one of the legs was shorter than the other."

"Yes, I know." He moved a few inches down the couch. "You know, Betty, the times I've wished I could have come back to see you. I've missed you so much."

"*Why* couldn't you? Why did you disappear like that, without a word or a goodbye to anyone? It was awful." Betty pursed her lips and crossed her arms. "You've caused us all a great deal of upset, you know…especially me."

Patrick's frown eased. "You missed me then?"

"Of course I missed you, you oaf!" Betty rolled her eyes. "And when I found out that a skeleton had been pulled out of the sea with one leg shorter than the other, I thought I was never going to see you again so you'll excuse me if I'm a little bemused. I mean, what are the chances of the remains of another man with a short leg being discovered in St. Eves? Goodness only knows who *that* is but the police are going to want to know that it's not you.

"Anyway, forget about that—what on *earth* is going on? *Why* did you disappear like that? And where have you been? And why have you forced your way into my home to steal that worthless painting? And *why* are you trying to keep your identity a secret?" She shook an angry finger at him.

Patrick held up his hands. "Alright, alright! Enough questions." He let out a great sigh and leaned back on the couch. "When I left here, I went to St. Matlock. That's where I've been for the last four years. But for the past five weeks, I've been staying at a bed and breakfast in St. Eves. And, purely by coincidence, the skeleton was found just after I arrived. I read about it in the paper."

"I see." Betty regarded him through narrowed eyes. "So are you going to tell me what's going on? And while you're at it, you can tell me why you never gave me those letters."

Patrick's head snapped up. "You know about them?"

"Yes, I know about them. Leo and Harriett moved to the bungalow you used to live in and found them under the floorboards. I even went to Sutton's Folly looking for you to give them back. Why did you leave them behind?"

Patrick's cheeks flushed and he rubbed his nose awkwardly. "Because when I moved to the other bungalow, I wanted a fresh start. You obviously weren't interested in me and having those letters around was just a constant reminder, so I left them

there. I didn't think anyone would ever find them,
though…not in my lifetime, anyway.

"I've thought of you often, Bet. You must have
known how I felt about you?"

Betty shook her head, the frustration clear in
the crease at her brow. "Well, it's a bit late to be telling
me now, isn't it? Honestly, I could shake you, Patrick
Jones. And heaven only knows what you've gone and
got yourself involved in, but it can't be anything
good—not with all this skulking around. So, come on
then, out with it. What's going on?"

He heaved a huge sigh. "Alright, I'll tell you, but
only because I think I owe you an explanation. But
then I'm leaving—and I'm not telling you where I'm
going." His shoulders hunched as he leaned forward
and began his story.

"I haven't been a good man, Betty—I'm a fraud.
I've kept secrets you wouldn't believe and I've lied to
you, and to everyone else. It wasn't *my* parents who
had money. It was my cousin's parents. They
emigrated to Canada years ago. They made sure my
parents were well provided for but, when they died,
they left everything to John."

Betty clicked her tongue in disapproval. "Well, I
don't understand why you felt the need to lie about it.
Who cared how much money you had, Patrick? Your
friends certainly didn't."

"*I* cared, Betty!" Patrick brought his fist down on the arm of the couch. "When I went to Canada, I assumed John would share his money with me—he had *so much* of it. But he didn't. He didn't even offer. He gave me a few hundred when I was running low, but I had to ask him for it. And then, he told me not to become accustomed to him giving me handouts because he wasn't going to. He said he'd give me a monthly allowance if I needed money. How do you think it felt to know that John had more money than he would ever spend when I had virtually nothing left except my pension?" In his fury, spittle flew from his mouth and his breathing became laboured.

Unsettled by his sudden change in mood, Betty chose her words carefully.

"Well, he must have thought a lot of you to have given you *some* money. It was good of him to give you *something*, don't you think?"

Patrick scoffed. "Oh, you think so, do you? Well, I don't. But I didn't come back from Canada completely empty-handed. I brought back a nice little insurance policy with me—eight gold and diamond rings and one of my uncle's Swiss watches. I took them from John's bedroom." He ignored Betty's look of horror.

"He had plenty more so I'm sure he wouldn't have missed them. In any case, he should have had them locked away in the safe if he didn't want them to get stolen. It served him right." His lips curled in a sneer. "They've certainly helped to keep my cash reserve topped up over the years."

"You stole from your own cousin?" Betty gasped. "I don't know what's happened to you but you're not the Patrick Jones I used to know."

Patrick glowered as he began pacing the room. "Oh, Bet, you don't know the half of it. The more I thought of John, sitting in his expensive house, in its exclusive neighbourhood, without a financial care in the world, the more I wanted to get my hands on him…and then one day, completely out of the blue, he called me. Said he was coming to see me."

Betty's eyebrow shot up. "What? Here? In St. Eves? Why didn't you introduce him to anyone?"

"You must be joking," Patrick scoffed. "He was the last person I wanted anyone to meet. I couldn't risk anyone finding out that I'd been lying to you all and John knew all about me. He knew I had no money, no family fortune—all the things I'd told everyone I had, John knew I didn't."

"Why did he come here? I thought you'd been on bad terms?"

"We had been, but he came to tell me he was ill. Said he'd known for over six months and had been getting things in order. He'd sold the family business and wanted to come over to see me because he knew he wouldn't get another chance. Said he wanted us to build bridges before he died, or some such nonsense, and that after he'd seen me, he was going to book a round-the-world trip while he still had the life in him to go on one. Before he did, though, he wanted to give me something. Well, of course, I thought he was going to sign the family fortune over to me. Or, at least half the proceeds of the sale of the business."

"And, did he?"

Patrick's laugh barely concealed his bitterness. "No, he didn't. He was going to leave all his money to an animal rescue centre in Ontario. Can you believe that? And do you know what he gave me?" He nodded to the bag on the couch.

"What, that painting?" Betty started to giggle. "Oh Patrick, I know I shouldn't laugh but that's so funny. I imagine you were disappointed?"

"Disappointed?" Patrick put his face close to hers. "I'll tell you how disappointed I was. I was *so* disappointed, I pushed him off the hilltop outside All Saints church."

Betty's smile faded. "What d'you mean, you "pushed him off the hilltop"?

"Just that." Patrick leaned back and crossed his legs. "I met him outside the church and we argued and fought. I hit him a few times and then I pushed him over the perimeter wall. It was very strange...everything went into slow motion and he just fell like a sack of stones."

Betty's hands flew to her mouth. "Oh, Patrick, you didn't..."

Patrick nodded his head. "I'm afraid I did, Betty."

"And you didn't call the police? Or an ambulance?"

"I didn't call anyone. If they'd been able to recover his body, the paramedics would have known straight away that we'd fought because I gave him such a pounding." He stroked his chin, thoughtfully. "I'm certain I broke his jaw. And I gave him quite a few bashes on the head with my walking stick. You know what forensics are like these days. I was scared that, if the body had been washed up, some of my DNA might have been found on it. I was scared, Betty, and I couldn't have coped with being locked up—not at my time of life. So I packed up and left. "

"So, the skeleton is John's?" Betty shuffled down the couch again, further away from Patrick. "But the dental records confirmed it was you. How is that possible?"

Patrick wagged a finger. "I told John to meet me outside the church because I knew we wouldn't see anyone I knew there. I drove up there and he arrived in a taxi, straight from the airport. He had two suitcases, his passport and all his papers in his travel bag. I remember it was warm that evening so he'd taken off his jacket and hung it over a bench.

"After John's 'accident', I went back to Sunny Days and looked through the suitcases. He'd brought his medical file with him—all his dental, doctor and optician records, along with his birth certificate and insurance documents. John was always very careful about his health and he wouldn't have wanted to go on a round-the-world trip without being prepared for every eventuality.

"When I realised I had his passport, his birth certificate, his medical records, his bank cards and his phone with all his contacts and online banking passwords saved on it, I decided to fake my own death so that I could never be blamed for John's.

"I went back to the church very early the next morning to check that the body hadn't been washed ashore and then I did a few last minute jobs in St. Eves before leaving in the middle of the night. I moved to a bed and breakfast in St. Matlock and made my plans. I *had* to leave St. Eves as I was convinced that if John's body was ever going to be found, it would be in the days soon after he fell. I scoured the papers every day, looking for news that his body had been washed ashore but when it wasn't, I guessed it had been taken with the current. When it hadn't been found after two months, I knew by then there was every chance it would pass for me if it was ever discovered. John and I didn't look similar but, as a skeleton, we probably were. We both had a short right leg, inherited from our fathers, and we both had bone spurs.

"I looked online and found someone who could make a falsified copy of an x-ray. It's amazing what people will do if you pay them enough—fake medical insurance claims are big business, you know, so it wasn't difficult to find someone who could do what I wanted.

"With my wig, beard and sunglasses, I wasn't worried about being recognised anywhere so I went to a dentist in St. Eves and told him I was having some pain in a tooth. He couldn't find anything wrong but I insisted he took an x-ray and told him I wanted a copy—told him I liked to keep records.

"Then I gave the guy I'd found online the x-ray of my teeth and the x-ray of John's teeth and asked him if he could put John's x-ray into the same format as mine, but with my name on it instead of his.

"When I got the x-ray back, I made another appointment at the dentist to have my teeth polished. I told the hygienist that I wanted the anaesthetic gel on my gums before the treatment because my teeth were sensitive. While that was taking effect for ten minutes, she went off and chatted to the receptionist, which I'd been banking on her doing as I'd seen her do the same thing while I'd been waiting to see the dentist the previous week. All I had to do while she was out of the room was switch the real x-ray of my teeth for the doctored x-ray of John's teeth with my name on it. Voila! John's dental records were now mine and, if the body was ever found, it would be identified as me. Clever, don't you think?"

Betty shook her head. "Crazy, more like. You've lost your mind."

Patrick ignored her. "Anyway, as soon as I'd swapped the x-rays over, that was the end of Patrick Jones. I threw my phone in the sea, stopped taking money out of my bank account—which, of course, made my disappearance and subsequent 'death' look more authentic—and started relying solely on the money in John's accounts, of which there was plenty." He laughed a self-satisfied laugh and ran a hand over his beard. "You know, wearing a disguise is very liberating. And I wish I'd never listened to my dad about not getting a lift for my shoe—it's fantastic. No more limping, no more aches and pains. And, of course, not having anyone recognise you is a perfect way to get away with murder."

"You weren't in disguise when you killed John, though, were you?" said Betty.

"No. But I was when I killed Gavin."

"What?!" Betty's voice rose to a shriek. "No, Patrick, please tell me you didn't!"

Patrick gave a little bow. "I'm afraid I did, although I can't take *all* the credit. It was the hornets that did the deed, you see. I just encouraged them into the box with a bit of paté and after I'd lured Gavin to the garden centre, I let them at him.

"You know, when he arrived, he didn't recognise me. I told him I was going to tell everyone that he'd been having an affair with Holly Simms for years. Told him I had some photographs of him and Holly in the box I had with me. Of course, he grabbed it from my hand, the lid came off, the hornets flew out and... Well, you know the rest."

"So it was you who wrote the note Charlotte found?"

Patrick nodded. "Guilty as charged. I left it under his windscreen wiper. Poor Gavin. You should have seen his face when those hornets went for him. They'd been in there for over an hour so they were pretty angry." He chuckled. "You should have guessed that a country boy like me would know all about the nocturnal habits of insects, Bet."

"But how did you know about his allergy?"

"Jemima told me about it years ago—something to do with his steroid use affecting his immune system. Anyway, he had it coming, it was nothing less than he deserved for treating Jemima the way he did. She was such a sweet girl—God only knows what she was doing with a thug like Gavin. When I was at Sunny Days, I offered to take him to one side and give him a piece of my mind many times, but she wanted me to stay out of it. She was scared that he'd turn on her if he knew she'd spoken to me about their relationship troubles."

"For heaven's sake! Thousands of couples have marital problems—why was it so important for you to get involved in Jemima's?"

Patrick's face fell, his sigh heavy. "Ah, you see, now that's a sad, sad story. I don't like to talk about it too much but, before we came to St. Eves, I had a sister. Her name was Lucy." As her name slipped from his lips, it was the only encouragement needed to coax a broad smile from them. "She was five years older than me and we were as close as two siblings could be." He took a creased photograph from his wallet. "Here, this is her a couple of years before she passed away."

Betty studied the picture of a young, dark-haired woman, being pushed on a swing and laughing to the camera. In Patrick's current mood, she had no intention of telling him that she already knew about his sister. "She's a very pretty girl. I'm so sorry, Patrick."

He shook himself. "Anyway, I've taught myself not to think about it too often now. I just get angry if I do."

"So, Jemima reminded you of your sister?"

Patrick shook his head. "*She* didn't, but her situation did. I couldn't be there for Lucy but I was damned if I was going to stand by and do nothing to help Jemima. After I came back, while I was watching your place, trying to decide when I should make my move, I saw her. I didn't expect to see her, mind you. I didn't think she'd still be at Sunny Days."

"And did she see you?"

"No. She and Gavin were unloading the car outside the office and he was yelling at her about something or other—poor kid, she looked so miserable. It made me so furious, Betty, I can't tell you. I just knew I had to do something about it." He rubbed at the furrow at his brow. "I couldn't understand why she was still with him—she should have left him years ago."

Betty stared at him. "Patrick, I'm so very sorry for what happened to your sister, but what's happened to *you*? Why have you turned into this murdering maniac? Since when did killing people become acceptable?" She clutched at her throat. "Oh my goodness! Am *I* next?"

She jumped up and rushed to the window, calling for help, but Patrick caught her before she had a chance to open the curtains.

"I'm sorry, I can't let you do that." He covered her mouth with his hand and pulled her back to the couch. "I've already told you, I don't want to hurt you but you're not making things easy for yourself. Now, please, just stay there and don't make a sound and I promise I'll leave you alone soon. I've got what I came for so as soon as that lot outside have cleared off, I'll be on my way."

Betty reached up her sleeve and pulled out a handkerchief. She blew her nose loudly and made a point of avoiding Patrick's gaze.

Minutes passed before she turned back to him. "Just a minute, why do you even *want* the painting if it's worth nothing?"

"Ah, well, you see, that's another story... After I left St. Eves, I went to St. Matlock, like I said, and rented a place in John's name using his money and his identification. After a week, I called his home and spoke to his housekeeper, Camilla—it wasn't difficult for me to sound like John—and told her that I was enjoying England, and catching up with my cousin so much, I'd decided to cancel my round-the-world trip and prolong my stay in the UK. Indefinitely."

"But how could he have stayed here for so long without anyone getting suspicious?"

"Because he had dual-nationality—he was born here, remember? "

"What about his mail? Surely it must have been mounting up back at his home in Canada?"

Patrick winked and clicked his tongue. "Thought of that, too. I asked Camilla to arrange for all the mail to be redirected to me at a PO box close to where I've been staying in St. Matlock."

"But didn't anyone ever try to contact him? His friends?"

Patrick nodded. "To start with, the damn phone never stopped ringing—thank God for caller ID so I could see who it was before I answered. I told everyone I'd decided to stay in the UK with my cousin and asked them all to give me some uninterrupted family time. And, do you know what? Not one of them realised it wasn't John they were talking to." He chuckled. "All things considered, I think I've managed everything very well."

"But why do you want that worthless painting?" said Betty. "And why have you decided to come back now, after all this time?"

"Well, believe me, it was never my plan to come back to St. Eves but if I tell you about the painting, you'll understand why I have. You see, when I went to visit John, I found out that my aunt and uncle had a safety deposit box which they locked away in a bank vault forty years ago. At the time, no one knew why they'd done it but they told John before they died that it was because they'd wanted his wealth to come from working the family business, *not* selling the family heirlooms, so they'd locked away some of their most valuable treasures for safekeeping for four decades. They wanted him to appreciate the value of money, you see."

"Well, it sounds like he did. It sounds like *he* had his head screwed on right," said Betty, scornfully. "Shame those principles don't run in the family."

Patrick clenched his fists for a moment, then relaxed. "Anyway, a letter from John's solicitor arrived last month telling him that now that the forty years had passed, he could open the box if he wanted to." Patrick's eyes glazed over with greed. "I don't know what's in there but I bet it's the family diamonds. My mum told me that aunt Ivy's mother had a jewellery collection worth millions.

"The letter said that, as per my aunt's and uncle's instructions, only the person with the secret six-digit password would be allowed access to the box. It was some kind of added security measure to make sure that only people who were entitled could open it. Only problem was, I had no idea what the password

was so I called the solicitor—I had no trouble
convincing him that I was John—and told him that I'd
prolonged my stay in the UK and had become too ill to
travel for the immediate future. I asked if it would be
okay if my cousin, Patrick, came to the bank to open
the box and asked what he'd need to bring with him.

"The solicitor said that would be fine. Said it
wasn't for him to say who could or couldn't open the
box, the only proviso as far as he was concerned was
that whoever it was, must be able to produce the
painting that contained the six-digit password before
he'd give them the key. Well, I knew then that it must
have been the painting John gave to me, that I gave to
you." He rubbed his hands together. "Thank God you
kept it, Bet. I can't tell you how much I'm looking
forward to a nice, long, holiday—first stop, Canada!"

Betty's jaw dropped. "So, are you telling me that
your poor cousin came all the way over from Canada to
give you a painting that's a key to a fortune worth
millions, and you killed him?"

Patrick shrugged. "Well, I didn't know that's
what it was, did I? He kept saying he wanted to go
somewhere and talk but I just wanted him to give me
whatever it was he'd come to give me, and clear off.
When he realised I wasn't interested in talking, he just
handed me a bag with the painting in it. He was

probably going to explain what it was but I was so mad when I saw it, he didn't get a chance."

"Well, I hope you're ashamed of yourself," said Betty. She stared around the room, deliberately avoiding him, and her eyes came to rest on the rectangle on the wall where Patrick had taken the painting from.

"Just a minute. That painting has been hanging on my wall since you gave it to me. There's no password on it. It's just a painting—just a jumble of swirls and straight lines." She grinned. "I think you've been taken for a fool, Patrick Jones."

He took the painting from the bag and examined it closely through a small magnifying glass on his keyring. True to Betty's word, there was nothing on it that even vaguely resembled a six-digit password.

He beat his fists against his head. "No, no, no! I've waited so long for this money…this must be the right painting, it must be!" His breath quickening, he ripped off the backing paper to search the back of the canvas but there was nothing. Furious, he flung it across the room, his face becoming redder and redder, the veins in his neck bulging bigger and bigger. The shock of realising the canvas wasn't the key to his million pounds retirement fund had tipped him over the edge.

"Oh, you must be enjoying this, Betty. You think I'm a fool, don't you?" He picked up a cushion and edged slowly towards her, his teeth bared in a crazed grin.

"No, of course I don't." Betty shrunk back in the couch. "I didn't say that *I* thought you were a fool. Now, Patrick, please, be reasonable—I won't breathe a word of any of this to anyone. Please—you're scaring me. Just leave and no one will ever know you were here."

"*You* said I'd been taken for a fool. I won't have you say that about me, not after I planned everything so meticulously. I don't know anyone who could have pulled off what I have and I won't let you say things like that. I just won't have it, Betty."

As he lunged forward, Betty screamed as loud as she could but he muffled the sound with the cushion over her face.

Everything happened so quickly.

The blaring sirens got louder and louder and then the front door flew open and Nathan, Ben, Fiona and a team of uniformed officers raced in.

Betty felt someone pull Patrick off her and then she heard Ben reading him his rights while Nathan handcuffed him.

"Patrick Jones, I am arresting you on suspicion of the murder of Gavin Campbell and John Jones and

the attempted murder of Elizabeth Tubbs. You do not
have to say anything but…"

"Okay, okay, you don't have to get all heavy-
handed," Patrick complained, as Nathan snapped the
handcuffs shut.

"*Heavy-handed*?" Ava appeared at the front
door, closely followed by Harriett. "I'll show you heavy-
handed, you thug," she said, before proceeding to set
about him with her handbag. "How dare you treat
Betty like this?"

"Ava, stop that at once, please," warned Nathan.

"Hmpf, I thought you'd be on *my* side." Ava
waited until he was looking the other way before
giving Patrick one more swipe with her handbag. She
watched him being escorted to a waiting police car
before turning her attention to Betty. "For heaven's
sake, how are you, dear?"

"I'm alright now that you've all turned up," said
Betty. "Thank goodness you got here in time—that
fortune teller's prediction was becoming a little too
true for my liking." She frowned. "Just a minute…
How *did* you get here in time? How did you know what
was happening?"

"Nora Tweedie, of course," said Harriett. "She
knew something was wrong as soon as she saw your
curtains were closed at half-past seven so she listened
through the air vent in the kitchen wall and heard

some of what was going on. She called Nathan and then she came round to tell me. Of course, I called Ava immediately and here we are."

Betty's jaw dropped. "Nora told you? And Nathan, too?"

"She certainly did. She thinks the world of you, Betty," said Nathan. "I just don't think she knows how to say sorry for behaving the way she has. It's not always easy to apologise, you know. Especially to the people who mean the most to us."

Betty nodded thoughtfully.

"Shall I put the kettle on?" said Harriett.

"Don't you dare," said Betty. "There's a bottle of brandy in the cupboard under the kitchen sink."

CHAPTER SIXTEEN

When Nathan got back to his office later that evening, he picked up his phone that he'd left on the desk and saw that there were twenty-one missed calls from Charlotte.

"Hi, you've been trying to get hold of me?" He held the phone away from his ear. "I'm sorry, I've been a bit busy this evening," he said, once Charlotte had got her concerns at not being able to contact him off her chest. "You've got a photograph of what? Oh, that could be very useful. Okay, I'll be home soon. You won't believe what I've got to tell you."

ooooooo

Nathan peered at the photograph, its colours dulled with age but still clear enough to show Patrick standing beside his father, each of them toasting the other with a glass of beer. In front of them sat Patrick's teetotal mother, a cup and saucer on her lap and two walking sticks leaning up against the chair. One was a traditional, wooden curved handle design, the other had ornate brass fittings and a handle in the design of a dog's head with a long muzzle and close-set ears.

"I think you're probably right, you know," said Nathan. "The handle looks solid and the dog's muzzle is just the right size and shape to have been responsible for Patrick's first, smaller head wound. He

told Betty that's what he'd used but we had no idea
what it looked like. I doubt we'll ever find it now but at
least we know what we're looking for when we search
his place in St. Matlock."

Charlotte sat at the end of the couch, her legs
stretched out over his lap.

"I just can't get my head around the fact that
Patrick's a double-killer. And that he went to all that
trouble with the dental x-rays to fake his own death.
And it was all for nothing. He didn't even find the
painting with the secret code." She shivered and
jumped up from the couch. "All this talk of murderers
is giving me the creeps. And you could probably do
with clearing your head. Come on, let's take the dogs
out."

ooooooo

"Anyway, I can't tell you how happy I am that
you've finally got a result. I know how difficult the
past few weeks have been."

Charlotte interlocked her fingers with Nathan's
as they walked the dogs.

"You and me both," he replied, reining in Panda
as he spied a handsome grey tabby cat sitting on a car
bonnet washing its paws. "I hope Betty's going to be
okay, though. The whole ordeal must have been a huge
shock for her."

"She's going to be fine, I'm sure. Ava called before we left home to let me know she'd been in touch with Dr. Talbot and he's dropping in to see Betty after surgery tomorrow, just to check her over. And Betty's going round to stay at Harriett and Leo's tonight so she won't be on her own. She's probably a bit spooked just now but I'm sure she'll be okay."

"Good. I'd hate for her to have any ill effects because of Patrick Jones. He's not worth Betty wasting a breath over, let alone feeling ill."

"I'll pop over tomorrow with Molly. Maybe we'll take her to St. Matlock if she wants to go. She likes the market they have there.

Nathan nodded. "Did I tell you? Patrick Jones is pleading innocence in all this. He swears he had nothing to do with either his cousin's or Gavin Campbell's deaths. Says it's only Betty's word against his and there's nothing to prove he was involved in either. When he was questioned after his arrest, he denied everything he told Betty. Said he must have been delusional." He rolled his eyes.

"But he's been impersonating his cousin and living off his money for the past four years. Is that not enough to prove he's guilty of his murder?"

"Well, it's enough to prove he's committed theft and fraud, certainly, but even though he admitted to Betty that he killed John, and we all believe him, without being able to place him at the scene of the crime, it's not as clear cut as you may think. And as for Gavin Campbell's death, we've got nothing that puts Patrick at the scene at all."

"What about what Nora Tweedie heard? Won't that help?"

"She heard enough to realise Betty was in trouble but nothing to incriminate Jones, unfortunately." A shrill ring issued from the depths of his jeans pocket. "Hang on a minute. DCI Costello. Yes. Oh, yes? Really? That's fantastic! Excellent news. We've got him! For the Campbell death, anyway. Thanks very much. Yes, you too."

"Good news, I take it?"

"They've just matched Patrick Jones' thumbprint to the partial print in the paté that was found in the box at the garden centre. And another print on the box has been identified as Gavin Campbell's."

"Well, you can't get much more proof that he was at the scene of the crime than that, can you? That's fabulous!"

"Agreed. I'd be a lot happier, though, if we could find something concrete to link him to John Jones's death, too."

"One thing at a time, Sherlock. Come on, let's go home."

"Indeed, Agatha. After you."

ooooooo

Two hours after he closed his eyes, Nathan woke with a start. Dreams filled with visions of skeletons, falls from great heights and being chased by killer hornets had done nothing to help lull him to sleep.

He slipped quietly out of bed and looked in on Molly on his way downstairs. "Good boys," he whispered when Pippin and Panda both raised their heads off the bed, one ear cocked, maintaining their night-watch over Molly.

He sat at the kitchen table with a cup of coffee. *How the hell are we going to pin John Jones's murder on Patrick?*

As he sipped his intense brew, he recalled the inscription on the headstone of the Jones family plot. *Let no hand touch the stones that keep, Flo, Henry and Lucy in heavenly sleep.*

"Hmmm, I wonder...."

ooooooo

The next morning, Nathan showed the photograph of the walking stick to Ben and Fiona and told them of his theory.

"It's the perfect place to hide a murder weapon and, if I'm right, it's been there since the night John Jones was killed."

"You think you'll get a licence?"

"I think so…I hope so, anyway. It's not as though I want the whole grave dug up. I just want the stones on top removed so the soil underneath can be examined. If they're careful, and I'll make sure they are, it won't even look like anything's been touched once everything's back in place. I could be completely wrong about this but my gut's telling me otherwise. And you know how I always like to follow my gut."

"Well, I haven't got a better suggestion," said Fiona, "and, at the moment, Patrick Jones is smugly thinking that we'll *never* find any evidence on him."

Nathan stood up. "If I needed any motivation to plead for this licence, that was it. We can't let Patrick Jones get away with this and I'm going to do everything I can to make sure he doesn't."

ooooooo

The Sunny Days club house was busy with the usual Saturday evening crowd, their gossip fuelled by news of recent events.

As Betty walked in, the chatter stilled and a hush fell over the room. She hadn't set foot in the club house since the evening she'd told Nora that Patrick had written the letters to her.

She scanned the room, her eyes searching for Nora and when she picked her out, at a table in a far corner sitting with Bea and Jocelyn, she headed straight for her.

"Oh my gawd, would you look who it is," crowed Bea as Betty drew near. "It's the heroine of the hour...I don't think."

"I hope you haven't come in here hoping to creep round Nora?" said Jocelyn. "In case you hadn't taken the hint over the past few weeks, she doesn't want to speak to you."

"No, she doesn't," said Bea. "And, quite honestly, I'd rather not be wasting my breath speaking to you either. So why don't you just do us all a favour and clear off? Ever since Nora..."

"No, Bea," Betty interrupted, her voice stern, "why don't *you* just do us all a favour and shut up?" Betty's stare bored into her. "I've got nothing to say to you, it's Nora I've come to speak to and I'm not leaving until I've said my piece."

Unaccustomed to anyone standing up to her, Bea shrivelled back in her seat, her lips clamped firmly shut.

Jocelyn opened her mouth and closed it again as Betty cut her dead with a glare of pure ice.

"Nora. You listening?"

Nora peered up through her eyelashes with a sheepish half-smile, and nodded.

"I won't outstay my welcome, but I heard what you did and I wanted to say thank you. If it hadn't been for you, I don't even want to think about what might have happened. I know things have been a little rocky between us recently but I hope you'll, at least, accept my gratitude." Betty gave her a little nod before turning and walking away.

"Wait! Betty, wait." Nora pushed her chair away from the table and rushed after her, her words tripping over themselves as they spilled from her lips. "I'm so sorry—I've behaved so badly, and all because I was jealous over a man. And a stupid pig of a man who was only interested in himself, at that. I can't believe I was so awful to you. You've been such a good friend." She bowed her head. "I really am sorry. Can you ever forgive me, do you think?"

Betty's dark eyes twinkled. "Oh don't be so daft. Of course I forgive you, you nitwit. Come here and give me a hug."

As Bea and Jocelyn massaged each other's bruised egos, Betty and Nora linked arms and retreated to another table.

ooooooo

"Come on, you two or we're going to be late. It would be nice if we could be there *before* Betty gets home from bingo, seeing as it's her surprise party. Ava just called to say everyone's arrived except us. Yes, Pip, yes, Panda, you're coming with us, don't worry." Charlotte bent to make a fuss of the dogs who rolled onto their backs with unfettered joy.

As was usual in the Costello household whenever even the shortest of trips was on the cards, Charlotte waited alone with the dogs while Nathan and Molly took their time getting ready, totally oblivious to deadlines and time frames.

She sighed and spritzed perfume into the air before walking through the mist twice and applying a smudge of rose-pink gloss to her lips. As she waited for the rest of her family, a smile turned up her mouth as she ran her hand over the pencil marks on the banister which had recorded Molly's growth over the years and she suddenly felt a lump in her throat.

"Mummy, do you think these shoes, or these ones?" Molly appeared at the top of the stairs, wearing a different shoe on each foot.

"Um, I think the ones with the bows, sweetheart."

"Oh." Molly's face fell. "But I like the ones with the pom-poms."

"Well, wear *them*, then. Just be quick about it." Charlotte sighed and checked her watch. "*Nathan!* Oh, there you are. You've been in the shower forever—what took so long?"

His eyebrow shot up. "Well, there's a lot of me to wash, you know." Pulling Charlotte to his hip, he dropped a kiss on her lips. "Have I told you how stunning you are? That dress looks fabulous."

"Thank you. And you look very handsome. And..."

"And what?" He interrupted, throwing her a broody stare. "Rugged? Sexy? Drop-dead-gorgeous?"

Charlotte smiled benignly. "And...you're standing on my hem."

"Hmmm?"

"My dress, you're standing on it."

"What? Oh, sorry." He stepped back and bumped into Molly who had changed her outfit completely, shoes included.

Charlotte raised her eyes and gathered her family in a hug. "Right, is everyone ready now? Yes? Then, let's go!"

oooooo

"Happy birthday to yoooouuuu!"

A round of applause broke out as Betty blew out the candles on her birthday cake.

"Thank you, everyone," she said, once the noise had died down. "This is such a surprise and it's so lovely to see you all. I usually only have a few crackers and cheese when I get back from bingo and you've all put on such a wonderful spread." She waved her hand across the table laden with goodies. "You know, there was a point not so long ago when—just for a moment—I wasn't sure I'd be here to celebrate this with you, so it makes it all the more special to see you here today.

You're my dearest friends and I honestly don't know what I'd do without you." She quickly blinked back the tears that pricked the back of her eyes. "Anyway, this is a happy occasion so I hope you'll all eat, drink, dance and enjoy yourself. Oh, and I'm going to cut this beautiful cake now, so please help yourself to a piece. Come on, Molly, love, you can have the first slice."

Molly's eyes widened as she took her slice of cake, along with Pippin and Panda, to the bean bag in the corner of Betty's living room which, as far as she was concerned, was "the coolest thing ever."

"I see they've made up then?" Nathan nodded to Nora Tweedie who was linking arms with Betty and wishing her all the best.

"Yes, I'm really glad they didn't let that business with Patrick Jones ruin their friendship," said Charlotte.

"What's going to happen to him, do you know?" asked Garrett.

"He's going to be locked up for a very long time," said Ben, as he twirled Jess around to a salsa beat. "And once we find something to pin his cousin's murder on him, once and for all, it'll be even longer."

"And what about Holly and Ellen, do you know?" asked Laura, filling her plate with salmon and salad.

"Well, for starters, they're going to pay the money back to the weight loss association. It's going to take a while but they've promised to pay back every penny—I'm pretty sure it'll end up in court. And, as you know, the Andersons have been replaced by new managers, so they won't be seen around here again."

"And what about Paul and Jemima?

"Well, there's another story. When Jemima found out the money came from stolen goods, she didn't want it. She wants to make sure it ends up where John wanted it to, so she's sending it all back. And Paul's learned his lesson, that's for sure."

"I'm surprised you've kept that painting, Betty." Leo waved his cake fork in its general direction. "I would have thought you'd be glad to see the back of it."

"Well, I did consider getting rid of it but I threw the letters out instead. I *like* the painting and I didn't want Patrick Jones to influence whether I kept it, or not."

"Good on you," said Harry. "Very wise." He raised his glass to Betty and gave her a wink.

"You know, I never for a moment thought that *John* Jones was the victim," said Betty. "Apart from the fact that no one had ever met him, we all thought that *he* was the perpetrator because of the lies Patrick had told everyone—that *John* had threatened to kill *him* after he refused to give him any money, not the other way round. Just goes to show, you never really know some people, do you?"

Charlotte looked over to where Molly sat on the bean bag, eating cake and staring intently at the picture above the fireplace.

"You alright, poppet?"

Molly nodded. "Betty," she said, munching on a mouthful of cake, "that picture on the wall, what's it supposed to be?"

"It isn't supposed to be anything, love, It's just shapes and swirls."

"What Betty means, dear, is that it's abstract," said Ava. "Which means that the artist has made little or no attempt to make it look anything like what it actually is."

"Oh." Molly nodded and licked icing off her thumb. "What are the numbers for?"

Numbers?" Betty looked up from cutting the cake, along with everyone else in the room.

"Yes, the numbers in the painting."

Betty put down the cake slice. "What numbers?"

Molly pointed to the painting and then across the room to the mirror on the opposite wall. "See, if you look in the mirror, you can see them."

The reverse image of the painting clearly showed a six-digit number skillfully disguised amongst the swirls and angles of the painting.

Doughnuts, Diamonds and Dead Men

"Can you believe it! How long have I had that painting hanging there and no one's ever noticed that. Molly, you're a marvel!"

"Good thing Patrick Jones didn't notice it. He would have cleared out his aunt and uncle's safety deposit box and ended up living the life of Reilly instead of paying for John's and Gavin's deaths," said Nora. "Honestly, I don't know what I ever saw in that man. He was a rogue. I mean, what kind of person thinks he's helping someone by getting rid of their husband? I ask you."

"Agreed," said Betty, and they clinked their champagne glasses together.

"Are you going to keep it?" asked Harriett.

"Well, I was going to but only if that doesn't prevent the contents of the safety deposit box from going to someone who should have it. Patrick mentioned that John had left all his money to some animal refuge so perhaps Nathan could arrange for someone to let John's solicitor know what's been going on. Then he can tell us what to do about it. I know Patrick said that anyone who had the password would be allowed to open the box but the family fortune is nothing to do with me—I don't want it. I'll speak to Nathan about it later.

"For now, though, someone put on some Bill Haley. I hope you've got your dancing shoes on, Harry—I feel a jive coming on!"

EPILOGUE

Early one morning, while mist still hung in the air and the grass was still damp underfoot, Nathan stood at the side of the Jones family grave as the white gravel was carefully removed and the top layer of turf sliced cleanly through to be removed in slabs.

Father Ryan, who had insisted that he oversee the proceedings, had kept up a stream of prayers and blessings throughout. "Oh, Nathan, I hope you're right about this. That metal detector didn't get a bleep, did it?"

"That's because brass is one of the hardest metals to detect. Don't give up hope yet, Reverend—for John Jones's sake."

He watched the as the soil was carefully sifted through, deeper and deeper down. After almost an hour with nothing having been revealed except roots and insects, he was beginning to give up hope himself until an object became visible through the silt.

"I think we've got something, DCI Costello."

ooooooo

"The blood on the walking stick is a match to John Jones, and Patrick Jones's DNA is all over it too. I'd say that's a result. Good work, everyone."

In the incident room, a rousing cheer went out and Nathan shook hands with each member of the team but, as he watched them celebrate he knew that, although justice would finally be done for John Jones, there was still one final part of his story to play out.

ooooooo

An emotional Camilla Santiago hugged Nathan and kissed him on both cheeks.

"Thank you for helping to bring Mr. Jones back to us. We are so thankful that we can bring him home now and lay him to rest with his parents."

John Jones's housekeeper had made the trip to St. Eves with her husband to accompany the remains of John's body back to Canada and had made a special request to meet the investigating team responsible for bringing his killer to justice.

From the contacts list on John's phone, Nathan had contacted his solicitor who had been in touch with Camilla and helped with all the necessary arrangements. He'd also told Nathan that Betty could keep the painting if she wanted to, as there was an overriding clause in John's will which said that if his parents' safety deposit box still hadn't been opened at the time of his death, the contents should be split equally between all his staff.

"You're very welcome," he said. "I'm happy that Mr. Jones is finally going back to where he was loved."

ooooooo

An Indian summer was blessing St. Eves with warm weather late into September—the perfect excuse for a late-season barbecue at the Costello home.

Gatherings at Charlotte and Nathan's were always a jolly affair. White lights and paper lanterns hung from trees, music played, drink flowed and there was always plenty of good food and great company.

"Ooh, I haven't had a chance to look at this yet. Better do it now before it becomes yesterday's news." Harry flicked through the pages of the morning newspaper as he munched on his burger. "Hey, Betty." He chuckled.

"What?"

"You want me to read your horoscope for you?"

"Harry Jenkins, you know what you can do with your horoscope, don't you?" Betty grinned as she bounced past to the music. "I never want to hear my horoscope again for the rest of my life, thank you very much."

As Molly invented a salsa dance routine in the corner of the garden with Esme and Erin, Nathan pulled Charlotte close to his side. "See this burger here, this big one, it's for you. I made it specially."

"Oh, did you now?"

"Yep, all for you. What do you want on it?"

"Um, let's see. Well, I fancy gherkins, ketchup, pickled beetroot, lots of fried onions,…"

"Okay, coming right up. And anything else?"

"And mushy peas."

Nathan stepped back and pulled a face. "Mushy peas? Who has mushy peas in a burger?"

"I can't help it. It's what I fancy." Charlotte put her hand over the top of her glass when Nathan pulled a wine bottle from a nearby cooler. "No thanks."

Ava bopped over, swaying to the music. "Hello dears," she said as she stepped lightly from foot to foot. "I love this song. He's one of my favourites, you know, Michael Bubble."

"You mean Bublé," Charlotte giggled.

"You know, strangely enough, some people actually *do* pronounce his name like that." Ava patted her on the cheek. "Anyway, I've just come to offer our services if you need a hand with handing out food, topping up drinks, or whatever needs doing, so if you need three willing waitresses, just shout."

"Okay, Ava, that's very kind but I think we'll be okay. You go and relax with the others."

"If you insist, dear, but..." She stopped mid-sentence as Nathan appeared from the kitchen with a green tin in his hand. "Nathan, what place do mushy peas have at a barbecue?"

"Don't look at me, Ava. It's what Charlotte wants." He put a spoonful of peas on the griddle to heat. "Gherkins, ketchup, pickled beetroot, fried onions and mushy peas. Not my cup of tea but it's what she fancies. Right, who's waiting for a hot dog? Come and get 'em, fresh off the grill!"

As Nathan rattled on, Ava's hands flew to her mouth.

"You're not...are you?"

Charlotte grinned and Ava threw her arms around her. "Oh, my dear, how wonderful!"

"What? What's wonderful? What's going on?" said Nathan.

Ava retreated to her seat, with a wink to Charlotte, and a finger to her lips.

"What's going on?" he repeated, handing Charlotte her burger.

"Oh, you know, not much. Just standing here, eating my mushy peas burger." She smiled and took a massive bite, closing her eyes as she savoured the mouthful. "Mmmm, that's delicious. Sure you don't want to try a bit?"

Nathan held up a hand. "No, thank you. I'm quite happy to have my burger the way I always do—lettuce, cheese, onions and mustard."

"Mmm, pass me that jar of pickled onions, will you?" She took a bite of her burger and then a bite of the crisp, vinegary onion. "Mmmm, oh my gosh, that's a match made in heaven."

"Charlotte, are you feeling okay?" Nathan eyed her with concern.

"Never better," she replied, as ketchup dribbled down her chin. "Can I have a serviette, please?"

"I don't understand why you've got such a thing for pickles all of a sudden." Nathan passed her a handful of serviettes. "You don't usually like anything with too much vinegar." He watched her devouring the burger. "Well, you did when you were pregnant, but that was just a craving, wasn't it? It wore off after Molly was born, didn't it?"

Charlotte nodded. "Uh-huh." She smiled and crunched into another onion.

Nathan's jaw suddenly dropped. Then he dropped his spatula and his hands went to his head. "Oh my God, you're not?"

She nodded, and blinked back a tear. "I am. Sorry Ava guessed before I'd told you. I thought she would when you started telling her about my burger."

"I don't care about that, Charlotte." Nathan kissed her. "I'm just so thankful that you haven't been taken over by some pickle-obsessed alien. Are you okay?"

"Yes, of course I am. I'm fine."

He stared at her for a long time. Then he laughed and rolled his eyes. "Oh my, here we go again…and I'm looking forward to every single minute." He kissed her. "I love you, Charlotte."

"And I love you," she replied. "And I hope you're ready for the biggest grilling we're ever going to get from Molly, who incidentally, will be expecting me to pop this little one out of my belly-button when the time comes."

Nathan raised an eyebrow and turned back to the barbecue with a grin. "Ah, well, as much as I'd *love* to be a part of that conversation, I've got an awful lot of burgers to flip…"

xx The End xx

Please sign up to my readers' group at http://sherribryan.com, if you'd like to receive a notification when further releases in my mystery series are published.

Each book contains a new mystery to solve, and is a stand-alone story, so they can be read in any order but, if you'd like to read them as they were written after this book, this is the order to follow.

TAPAS, CARROT CAKE AND A CORPSE – Book One
FUDGE CAKE, FELONY AND A FUNERAL – Book Two
SPARE RIBS, SECRETS AND A SCANDAL – Book Three
PUMPKINS, PERIL AND A PAELLA – Book Four
HAMBURGERS, HOMICIDE AND A HONEYMOON – Book Five
CRAB CAKES, KILLERS AND A KAFTAN – Book Six
MINCE PIES, MISTLETOE AND MURDER – Book Seven

Doughnuts, Diamonds and Dead Men

A SELECTION OF RECIPES FROM DOUGHNUTS,
DIAMONDS AND DEAD MEN

Easy Doughnuts

Ingredients (Makes 24)

Dry ingredients

2 cups plain (all-purpose) flour, sifted

¼ cup sugar

1 tablespoon baking powder

1 teaspoon salt

1 teaspoon nutmeg or cinnamon

Wet ingredients

¼ cup vegetable oil

¾ cup milk

1 egg

1 teaspoon vanilla extract

Oil for frying

Sugar for serving

Method

1. Measure dry ingredients into a bowl and mix together.
2. Add all wet ingredients, apart from the oil for frying
3. Heat oil to 170°C in a deep fat fryer. (Some people will tell you that 180°C is better but I tried that and the outside got too brown before the inside was cooked).
4. When the oil is ready, use two tablespoons spoons to drop the batter into the oil. Don't drop it from too high up or it'll splash back. You're looking for the batter to bubble gently around the edges, not fiercely.
5. Let the doughnuts cook for about two minutes each side.
6. Remove from oil, drain and roll in sugar while still hot.

Note; I'd recommend that you try one first. Cut it open when you think it's ready and check the centre. If it's still a little uncooked, cook the next one for a few seconds longer.

Strawberry Cheesecake

Ingredients

For the base

2 cups porridge oats

3 tablespoons sugar

½ cup unsalted butter, melted

For the filing

2 x 8oz pack cream cheese

½ cup icing sugar

1 teaspoon vanilla extract

2 eggs

For the topping

10 oz ripe strawberries (Or other fruit—raw or cooked—of your choice. If you prefer you can use syrup, chocolate shavings, etc.)

An 8" lined foil or other ovenproof dish with raised sides

Method

1. Heat oven to 165°C
2. Line your dish with non-stick baking paper
3. Mix the oats, sugar and melted butter together well and use to line the dish.
4. Mix together the cream cheese, icing sugar, vanilla and eggs until just combined.
5. Pour the filling onto the base in the dish.
6. Bake for 45 minutes. The centre should still be a little wobbly but this will firm up as it cools.
7. Leave until completely cool before chilling in the fridge overnight, or for at least four hours.
8. Decorate with toppings of your choice and serve with cream.

Mango and Kiwi Mocktail

Ingredients

1 carton mango juice

2 fl oz sparkling water

4 fl oz kiwi juice

Ice cubes

A few splashes grenadine

Kiwi slices to garnish

Method

1. Add everything to a large jug, except the grenadine.
2. Mix together well.
3. Pour into glasses.
4. Carefully add a few drops of grenadine.
5. Garnish with kiwi slices and serve.

A Note from Sherri

Hi, and thanks for getting this far!

If you're a newcomer to the series and this is the first book you've picked up, you may like to know that book one in the series, *Tapas, Carrot Cake and a Corpse,* is free to download.

However as each book is a story in its own right, you shouldn't miss out on too much by reading them out of sequence if that happens to be the case.

If you haven't yet read the other books but would like to, may I suggest that, for the benefit of continuity, you start with *Tapas, Carrot Cake and a Corpse* followed by *Fudge Cake, Felony and a Funeral, Spare Ribs, Secrets and a Scandal, Pumpkins, Peril and a Paella, Hamburgers, Homicide and a Honeymoon, Crab Cakes, Killers and a Kaftan and Mince Pies, Mistletoe and Murder*

You may, of course, read the books in any order you wish, but if you'd like to read them in the order they were written, then *Tapas, Carrot Cake and a Corpse* is where to get started.

As with the other books in the series, which have been proofread and edited numerous times, there may still be the odd mistake within its pages. If you should come across one, I'd really appreciate you letting me know so I can I can put it right.

You can contact me by email at sherri@sherribryan.com, on Twitter @sbryanwrites or on Facebook at https://www.facebook.com/sherribryanauthor.

If you'd like to receive news about forthcoming books, along with details of free downloads from time to time, please visit my website at http://sherribryan.com, where you can also sign up to my readers' list. Please don't worry, I respect your privacy and I promise I won't bombard your inbox with messages or junk mail, nor will I ever share your name or email address with anyone! (Incidentally, if you would like to, you can now also sign up to my readers list directly from my Facebook page by clicking on the 'Sign Up' button).

Thank you again for taking the time to read my book, and this message.

Until next time, sending you very warm regards,

Sherri.

ABOUT SHERRI BRYAN

Sherri lives in southern Spain with her husband and her rescue dog.

If she's not tapping away on her keyboard, you'll either find her with her nose in a book, creating something experimental in the kitchen, playing with the dog or dreaming up new cozy mystery plots.

DEDICATION

To you, and everyone who has read the Charlotte Denver series—a huge thank you for your support.

And to Joyce, Rolo and Tom, all of whom were much loved, and who went to fly with the angels while this book was being written. You are missed.

"May your spirits soar high and free,
May your love be ever present,
May we keep you always in our hearts,
And may God keep you close in His kingdom."
Sherri Bryan - 2015

Sherri Bryan

Published by Sherri Bryan · Copyright ©2017

Doughnuts, Diamonds and Dead Men

33417225R00171

Printed in Great Britain
by Amazon